OUTER BANKS TALES
TO REMEMBER

OUTER BANKS TALES TO REMEMBER

by CHARLES HARRY WHEDBEE

JOHN F. BLAIR, Publisher
Winston-Salem, North Carolina

Second Printing, 1986

Library of Congress Cataloging in Publication Data

Whedbee, Charles Harry.
  Outer Banks tales to remember

    1. Outer Banks (N.C.) — History — Local — Addresses,
essays, lectures. 2. Legends — North Carolina — Outer Banks.
I. Title.
F262.096W475   1985   975.6'1   85-1300
ISBN 0-89587-044-4

Again, to ℛACHEL

FOREWORD

THE SMALL VOLUME you hold in your hand is the fourth in a series of such books. In each book, the writer, inspired by a deep and lasting love, admiration, and respect for the stalwart souls who brought civilization to North Carolina's Outer Banks, has tried to preserve a portion of the priceless heritage handed down through the generations by word of mouth.

Efforts have been made to substantiate these tales, where possible, by research and documentation. However, the unverified stories, too, are entitled to respect, told as they are by sincere and honest people.

Whether you believe any or all of them, a tale should be, like beauty, its own excuse for being. Almost everybody, young and old alike, enjoys a good yarn. So take these as fact or take them as fiction. Each is a part of Americana and is as much a part of our Outer Banks as Jockey's Ridge itself.

God rest you merry!

Charles Harry Whedbee

Whalebone Junction
Nags Head, N.C.

CONTENTS

PETER PAINTER'S REVENGE

*F*OR MANY GENERATIONS before the American Revolution, the Outer Banks of North Carolina were populated by a sturdy, honest, and almost fearless people, mostly of English stock.

Although these early settlers were fishermen for the most part, some pursued other occupations. Some were merchants, with small shops in places like Ocracoke and Portsmouth. Others were, quite frankly, pirates. These "Brethren of the Coast" were not held in low regard. Many of the merchants and some of the other residents depended on them for the material things that made life a little easier. Like smugglers, they were regarded as a source of necessities as well as some luxuries, and they were at least as honest as many of the merchants in places such as Portsmouth, who were believed to cheat and steal from the honest fishermen at every opportunity.

While there exists scant written history about the region in those days, many of the fisher families still survive, and they remember the tales handed down from grandfather to grandson. It is a folk history which is theirs alone. While it is most probable that these stories have been embellished somewhat in the telling and retelling down the generations, the majority of them are surprisingly accurate and check out with what bits of written history do exist. They are usually prefaced with an expression such as "the old folks say" or "my great-grandfather once told me."

One such story, which is greatly beloved and frequently retold, is the narrative of Peter Painter's revenge.

That Peter Painter actually existed in the late 1600s and early 1700s there can be no doubt. His name does appear in the colonial records of that day. However, it is the gaps in his recorded history that make Mr. Painter fascinating.

People say (and the records agree) that Peter Painter was a pirate, and a very successful one. He knew his business well. The small, swift, and easily maneuvered boats he preferred allowed him tactical advantages over the usually large and clumsy merchant ships that were his prey. It is said that he never flew the skull and crossbones flag or the black flag so commonly associated with piracy. His ensign was a blood-red battle flag, which he displayed whenever he was going into action.

Legend has it that Painter was also a humane pirate, within limitations. There is no reason to believe that he ever made anyone walk the plank, and he is said to have offered captured seamen the chance to serve with him as pirates if they chose. If they refused, he would not have them killed. He would simply maroon them on some deserted coast and sail away with their boat and cargo.

One exception to this procedure occurred whenever Painter captured a slave ship. According to folk history, Painter would free the slaves from their chains in the holds. As the pirates watched and cheered, the freed men would then rush up on deck and proceed to kill the

2

captain and the crew of their former floating prison. That done and the bodies heaved overboard, Painter would give the ex-slaves a few basic instructions in navigation and ship handling, after which he would sail away in search of more profitable prey. Many of the slaves were from the island of Jamaica, and some of them were wise in the ways of the sea and could handle their new-found vessel competently. Though some of them perished, others made it back to Jamaica, and a few no doubt turned pirate on their own.

Captain Painter's home was in Portsmouth Town on Portsmouth Island in what is now Hyde County, North Carolina. He was held in rather high regard there. He never caused any trouble ashore, and he kept his word with the local merchants and the other coastal residents as well as with his own crew members. He was a pirate and the people knew it, but they did not fear him. He is said to have helped many people in need and in trouble, sort of a one-man welfare department. Ashore, he behaved himself and was a good citizen—a good deal better than some. What he did when he was at sea was his business, and most people did not try to pry into it.

Painter's happy hunting ground was the Caribbean Sea, and his home away from home was the notorious pirate town of Port Royal on the island of Jamaica in that sea. This small city was a phenomenon not seen before or since in this hemisphere.

Christopher Columbus discovered the island of Jamaica on the morning of May 3, 1494, and he was greatly impressed with the beauty and charm of the place. He anchored in what was later to be the Port Royal harbor and took possession in the name of the royal government of Spain. From that time the island changed hands a number of times as the unsuccessful Dutch, the frustrated French, and the eventually victorious British all tried in turn to conquer and to hold the verdant land. The English finally solidified their hold in 1655, and the island has been British ever since.

In terms of actual government, however, the pirates took hold of the town of Port Royal and ruled that city for years. The story of how Henry Morgan, pirate extraordinary, first came to power is a strange one.

In the 1670s, Morgan sailed from Jamaica with a large fleet of pirate ships and burned and sacked Spanish Panama City, bringing away treasure that totalled, even in that day, in the millions of dollars. It made no difference that Spain and England were at peace and that Madrid's protests against the piracy were loud and long. Morgan was tried, but not only was he acquitted, he was actually knighted for his feat and was named by King Charles II as deputy governor of Jamaica in November, 1675. He returned to Port Royal in triumph and soon greatly enlarged the size and power of the pirate population of the town.

That lovely city became the most wide-open, rip-roaring center of debauchery you could imagine. One reliable report of the time estimated that for every one hundred people in Port Royal, there were at least fifty establishments that sold strong drink. Even then Jamaican rum was famous, and the pirates guzzled it with abandon. Prostitutes were encouraged and were on hand by the hundreds, plying their ancient profession where they chose. Many of them returned to England

4

rich beyond belief after a few years. Public drunkenness was the accepted norm, and fist fights and duels were an everyday occurrence. So long as the pirates paid their bills, they could do just about anything they pleased without let or hindrance.

This unusual system was administered and enforced by a governing group composed entirely of pirates, and Sir Henry Morgan was the chief pirate. His word was law, and he sat as both judge and jury, but he was consistent. Mutiny was punishable by death on the gallows. Debt was punished by long and sometimes indeterminate prison sentences.

The chief revenue of this administrative body was a port tax that was imposed on each incoming pirate ship. The captain of such a ship was required to pay a small percentage of the value of his entire cargo. For that port fee or tax he was allowed the freedom of the city, plenty of room to careen and repair his ship, all the rum he could pay for, and protection from the British authorities. It was truly a pirate sanctuary run by pirates for pirates, and it roared with revelry both night and day.

This, then, was Captain Peter Painter's vacation spot. The North Carolina pirate visited there often. It was conveniently close to the sea lanes used by the Spanish treasure ships and offered refuge in time of storm or of pursuit by a superior force.

Sir Henry Morgan ruled for awhile but had the bad judgment to immerse himself in the rowdy life of the city he ruled. In spite of the gout and stern warnings from his doctors, he practically lived in the so-called pot houses of the town and literally drank himself to death, dying of liver disease in late 1688. He was fifty-three years old.

Upon the death of the old pirate, the governing power of the city passed to a group of pirates headed by the infamous Red Legs Graves. This worthy earned the name "Red Legs" because of the savage way he used his cutlass when boarding a ship. It was said that the decks of such ships ran red with the blood of his slaughtered adversaries until he was stained almost to his hips with their gore. This was the man who had taken Sir Henry Morgan's place as the actual ruler of Port Royal.

It was in 1692 that Captain Painter returned to this city, unaware of the changes in the pirate government. No sooner had he gotten into town and gotten drunk than he was clapped into jail on a charge of not paying his port fee. The captain was furious. He knew full well he had paid his entry fee, but he could not find his receipt. Although he was well known in the town and respected among the other pirates, his protests against the new administration were in vain. He was tried quickly and as quickly sentenced to remain in prison until he paid five times the port fee for his vessel.

The visiting pirate might well have stayed in that stinking prison for the rest of his life had not his quartermaster and several of his crew gotten together and sold what remained of their share of the last conquest to raise money to pay him out. As soon as he was out of jail, Captain Painter lost no time in setting sail toward the west.

Once out of the harbor and well away from the island, the outraged captain walked to the rail at the stern of his quarterdeck. Shaking his clenched fist at the city in the distance, he swore an awful pirate oath. The story goes that he actually called on the devil himself and all the evil spirits of the undersea world to avenge his treatment, promising to serve the devil the rest of his days in return.

Even as the crewmen watched in terror, there came an awful rumbling from the very depths of the sea. The ocean became violently agitated with waves running in every direction and colliding with each other in confusion.

Ashore, a violent earthquake shook the island of Jamaica from end to end. Before the eyes of Painter's crew, the city of Port Royal suddenly sank beneath the sea, lock, stock, and barrel. It just disappeared as though some giant sea creature had swallowed it up. Where the town had been, the turbulent sea was dotted with the struggling figures of men and women drowning. Boats were capsized like so many toys. The whole town was destroyed, and the human survivors were few indeed. A tremendous tidal wave followed the earthquake, but it caught Captain Painter's ship squarely on her high stern and the vessel somehow managed to ride up and over the huge surge without loss of life. The entire crew escaped to the open sea.

This was Peter Painter's revenge. History records the earthquake and the complete destruction of Port Royal. The folklore of the coastal people to this day describes the event as the pirate's revenge, and it has been so handed down through the years from generation to generation.

What became of Captain Peter Painter after that?

Well, in March of 1701, King William proclaimed an "Act of Grace" offering pardon for all piracies committed prior to that date, provided the outlaws would surrender and take an oath of allegiance to the Crown within twelve months.

Having accumulated enough wealth to last the rest of his life, Peter Painter immediately took up with this proposition. He came in and confessed his sins and took the oath. For some reason, though, no pardon was forthcoming.

In August of 1701, according to the *Journals of the Assembly*, Peter Painter, citizen, was recommended for appointment to the important position of public powder receiver under His Majesty's government. His appointment was flatly refused by the upper house. Governor James Moore wrote to the House of Commons reporting, "Mr. Painter, having committed Pyracy and not having his majesties pardon, he is considered unfit for the post and his petition is refused."

What happened after that is obscured by the mists of the past. Some say that Painter returned to his home in Portsmouth Town and lived out his days in affluence. Others say that, disgusted by the refusal of the promised pardon, he resumed his piratical ways until his death.

Edward Teach, better known as Blackbeard, did not come on the scene until several years later, but he operated in the same general area and in the same general manner. He was killed aboard his ship in November of 1718 in what is now known as Blackbeard's Hole in the sound near Ocracoke, and just a short distance from Portsmouth Town. The list of his crewmen killed in that encounter with Lieutenant Maynard of Virginia includes the name "P. Paynter." The spelling is a little different, but the pronunciation is accurate for the time and place.

Could this be our Captain Peter Painter?

Whether or not he died at that time and place and in that manner, the story of Peter Painter's revenge will live on as long as there are grandfathers on our coast to tell a tale while the winter gale howls outside, and wide-eyed Banker children to listen spellbound to the tales of long, long ago.

THE FABLE
OF THE COBIA

*E*VERY SERIOUS saltwater fisherman knows and respects the cobia. The commercial fisherman knows him as a strong and active fish who can, and sometimes does, wreak havoc with a net. The angler admires him as a stubborn and spirited fighter on the other end of a line who can test his skill and endurance to the utmost. To both he is a prized quarry to be sought after and talked about, both before and after the catch.

The hook-and-line sportsman as well as the crews of the charter boats that ply the waters off North Carolina's Outer Banks know something else about him. They know that in the majority of instances, when you go after cobia, you will see not just one but two of them. In a great many instances, if one fish is boated, you will soon see another of approximately the same size circling the boat. Sometimes, it is said, the second fish will actually jump into the vessel, but usually it just circles around and around the boat until the fishermen leave the scene. They are rarely seen as singles or in threes or fours, and they do not seem to be a school fish.

Ichthyologists, who know the fish as *Rachycentron canadus*, are at a loss to explain this peculiar circumstance, but the ancients knew. To them the reasons were perfectly clear.

Long, long ago, when the sea was young and the earth was very new, things were different from what they are now. Neptune was the ruler of the ocean depths. Although he was also very young, he ruled with a fair and impartial hand, and all the creatures of the sea respected and loved him.

That is, almost all of them.

Then, as now, the devil made frequent trips into the depths to try to extend his kingdom of evil. He greatly resented the young Neptune's reign over so many subjects.

The Evil One had a few allies, such as the Mako sharks, certain octopuses, and most stingrays, but he longed to extend his power to rule over all the sea creatures. Toward that end he began to lay his plans.

Satan knew that, to begin with, he must find some way to capture or otherwise neutralize Neptune. But what could lure him into a trap? The ocean king seemed to have everything he could want. Gold and precious jewels he had in plenty, and food and raiment were available to him in great variety.

The one thing the ruler seemed to lack was love. Although he was young and strong and very handsome, there was no feminine counterpart to share his rule, and he was often lonesome. This loneliness the devil saw as the Achilles heel by which he might successfully capture the king.

Using one of his favorite tactics, Satan changed the form of a certain voluptuous octopus into that of the loveliest mermaid you can imagine. Although she was still an octopus at heart, she now had long, blonde hair, and eyes the color of a sunlit Carolina sky. Her smiling lips opened to show her pearly white teeth, and her figure was literally out of this world. This was the bait with which the Prince of Darkness hoped to lure young Neptune into captivity.

Deep beneath the ocean, Satan then prepared a large cave lined with huge rocks several feet thick. The opening to the cave was closed by a gate of iron bars as thick as a man's thigh. This gate slid back on a track behind the wall of the cave, and so was cleverly concealed when open. Inside the cave the Evil One ensconced his mermaid on a soft bed of seaweed. Light from phosphorescent candles bathed the whole scene with an inviting glow.

How Neptune was lured to this particular spot on the ocean floor is not known, but come by he did, and in his youth and loneliness, he fell victim to the trap. He entered the open door of the inviting grotto intending to become acquainted with the vision of loveliness he saw inside. The iron-barred gate slid shut with a snap! Her work accomplished, the false mermaid then turned back into an octopus, and she slithered easily between the iron bars and back to the open sea.

The sea king was caught! The lock on the gate held fast in spite of all his pounding, and his cries for help were drowned out by the mocking laugh of Satan as he relished his victory. Now, he thought, he could proceed with his plan to become the undisputed ruler of the deep.

Neptune was desolate. He had been trapped by a simple trick, and he was furious with himself for having fallen for such a ruse. Only his extreme youth and the loveliness of the creature who had attracted him could have combined to humiliate and trap him so. Nevertheless, trapped he was.

Being a gentleman, the sea king had left his trident outside when he entered the cave, and he had no tool or pry-bar with which to attack the lock on his prison. He stretched his muscular arms as far as he could through the bars and tried to reach his trident, but it was just beyond his reach. He threw himself upon the bed of seaweed and shook his head in frustration.

Just at that dark moment, two cobia appeared on the scene and looked through the gate at the unhappy king. He told them of his plight and asked for help in recovering his trident. Now, one of the fish could not do it alone, but between them, they managed the job. While one fish turned the trident up on its side so that it would go between the bars, the other pushed and pushed on the other end until the tines of the trident slid between the bars and into Neptune's grasp.

With that magical tool once more in his possession, the sea king took only a moment to pick the lock of his prison and was once again a free being.

Turning to the two fish, he told them that he would grant them a special status, which would be unique among all the dwellers under the sea. As a mark of his gratitude, the cobia for all time would be the only fish in the deep that would mate for life. In their natural state they would be found in pairs and only in pairs for all time.

This is the story that the ancients knew and handed down to their children and their children's children, until somehow it became part and parcel of seaside folklore. There was even a time when some fishermen would not keep a cobia if they caught one. With a whispered aside to the king of the deep, they would unhook the fish and throw it back into the ocean to rejoin its mate and swim away, no doubt being scolded by that mate all the while for being stupid enough to fall for the fisherman's lure in the first place.

HOW OREGON INLET
GOT ITS NAME

*T*HE VARIOUS INLETS that pierce the Outer Banks of North Carolina have been the subject of much interest since long before the white man first set foot on this continent. Indians and early navigators alike relied upon the inlets for ingress and egress to and from the American mainland, always with the awareness that these routes were subject to change without notice. Throughout history, these gateways to the sea have moved and shifted, opened and closed and reopened and reclosed times without number. The inlet named Oregon is a case in point.

A map prepared in 1585 by John White, governor of Sir Walter Raleigh's so-called Lost Colony, shows an inlet at a place White called "Fort Fernando," approximately the same location as that of the present Oregon Inlet. About 1733 the same inlet appears on a map by Edward Moseley but is named Gun Inlet, which is the same name given the opening on John Collet's map dated 1768.

A few years later, however, the inlet had completely closed and was no longer shown on any maps. At the turn of that century, the Outer Banks are said to have been at least a mile wide at the point of the former inlet, with a thick growth of merkle bushes and cedar trees reaching a height of ten or fifteen feet.

Such was the situation in 1846, when Captain Jonathan Williams was sailing out of Edenton, North Carolina. The little town at that time was known as the Port of Roanoke, and it had all the color and excitement of a cosmopolitan world trade center, with almost daily ship arrivals from Boston, New York, and the West Indies. It was a happy home for Captain Williams and his three unmarried sisters, all of whom lived at the Williams plantation. While their brother sailed to faraway ports, Miss Harriet, Miss Tabitha, and Miss Penelope Williams led an orderly and peaceful life on the mainland, running the plantation and engaging in the pleasant social life of the town.

On the morning of September 3, 1846, Captain Williams conned his square-rigged sailing vessel, *Oregon,* away from the docks at Hamilton, Bermuda, down the broad waters of Great Sound, and out into the open Atlantic Ocean. The vessel carried a mixed cargo of cotton, tobacco, onions, several barrels of whale oil, and a quantity of highly prized juniper lumber known as "Bermuda cedar." Although New York was his destination, Captain Williams set his course west by south and pointed directly toward Cape Hatteras some 580 miles away in order to pick up the northward push of the Gulf Stream to speed him on his way.

The weather did not suit Captain Williams nor his first mate, Ahab Mann. The sky was a clear, bright blue, but the barometer had been dropping steadily, and the waves, once the *Oregon* reached the open sea, were the largest the captain could remember seeing. It seemed to him that an ominous sense of foreboding filled the ship and the members of its crew as though some awful thing

16

were about to happen. Even then the legend of the Devil's Triangle was known to men of the sea.

As the schooner sailed ahead, the weather grew steadily worse. The wind increased to a full gale and clouds of black scud began to appear in ragged festoons driving across the sky. What had been a favorable wind now increased to a dangerous gale, and Captain Williams had to order shortened sail and lifelines rigged across his decks to keep his crew from being swept overboard by the huge waves that occasionally broke over the decks.

And then the rains came.

Beginning as a misty drizzle, the rain increased from day to day without letup until it seemed as though the very floodgates of heaven had been opened to allow an almost solid torrent of water to pour into the hapless ship. It was impossible to see the bow of the vessel from the helmsman's position at the wheel. Driven by the raging wind, the downpour seemed almost horizontal rather than vertical. The torrential rains seemed to do nothing to flatten the raging sea, which rose and towered in ever-heightening mountains of tortured green and white water. The sun was blotted out and the deluge continued in semidarkness.

By September 7, Captain Williams was completely lost. He knew his schooner should be somewhere between Bermuda and the dangerous waters of Cape Hatteras, but as to his exact location and the distance to the deadly cape, he could only guess. Dead reckoning was impossible.

Records of the voyage of the U.S. brig *Washington*, caught in the same storm some miles to the north, describe the desperate situation. John F. Sanders, writing in the University of North Carolina Sea Grant College Program in an article entitled "The Hurricanes That Opened Oregon Inlet," quotes a young naval officer on the *Washington* as follows: "... sea and current drove the vessel upon (toward) Cape Hatteras... the gale, now increased in volume, howled ominously through the rigging, and already our little vessel swaggered under her canvas; the sky was obscured by flying masses of dark clouds; the crests of the waves heaving their dark volumes to the sky, flashed with the ghostly phosphorescent light often observed in storms... the barometer fell rapidly, and everything foretold a terrible strife of the elements."

During the night the wind had increased to hurricane force. All the small boats on the brig were crushed. The jib, topmast and staysail were lost, and... "the brig lay over completely on her side; the water boiling over the lee rail." For hours the crew held to the rigging, but "... a heavy sea broke on board... washing overboard nearly every soul. In a moment they were swept from our view; that moment showed them calm and composed, the determined spirit which supported them on board seemed still to animate them. One noble fellow as he passed astern waved his hat in token of adieu, and the driving spray hid them forever from our sight."

Closer inshore, Captain Williams also lost every sail except his shortened mainsail and jib. With each towering wave that overtook them from astern, it seemed as though the laboring *Oregon* would be completely swamped and lost with all hands. Captain Williams fully expected each moment to be his last upon this earth, and brave man though he was, his heart and brain were filled with terror. Taking firm hold on the lifeline rigged across the deck, the skipper dropped to his knees beside the two helmsmen struggling to keep the vessel under some sort of control. He prayed with complete sincerity for guidance and for salvation from a sea gone completely mad under the scourge of the screaming wind.

At the same time and far inshore, the Port of Roanoke was feeling the sting of the hurricane also. Later in the month the *Edenton Sentinel* was to report: "Much damage has been done by the late storm to the shipping on the coast. Our Bay (Edenton Harbor) presented quite a novel appearance; nearly all the water was blown out of it, except immediately in the channel. The water in Perquimans River, near Hertford, fell seven feet, which was, as a gentleman living in that vicinity informed us, four feet lower than he had ever known it before. At Nag's Head the tide rose about nine feet higher than common tide, and destroyed the warehouse of Mr. Russell, proprietor of the Hotel, together with all the stores which it contained, carrying it down the Beach about half a mile, swept away the market house; the house belonging to Dr. Wright was blown from its blocks; and nearly all the trees on the Hill were destroyed. Several families were compelled, for safety, to leave their houses and seek shelter in the Hotel. All the boats belonging to this place were carried off, depriving them of the means of fishing for a time. Persons living some four miles below Nag's Head, on the sea beach, found it necessary to flee to the garrets of their houses; to save themselves from drowning. They lost all they had to survive on—their clothing was all destroyed, and also their cooking utensils."

Out on the Williams plantation, the three sisters were fast asleep although the great house, as they called it, was shaking and trembling under the impact of the rising wind. The trees lining the lane to the house were leaning sharply away from the force of the gale.

As she told it later, it was on the stroke of midnight that Miss Penelope, the youngest sister, was awakened from her deep slumber by a voice calling her name over and over again. As she sat up in alarm, a blue light seemed to suffuse her bedroom and she could see quite clearly the form of her long-deceased mother standing at the foot of her bed. "Penelope, Penelope," the spirit moaned, "your only brother is in mortal peril on the sea and even now he stares into the jaws of death. Pray, girl, pray!" As suddenly as it had appeared, the apparition vanished, along with the eerie blue light.

Terrified, Penelope sprang from her bed, and without pausing to make a light, she dropped to her knees. She had always been a serious and devout young woman, believing that God spoke directly to human beings if they would only listen. Now she knew He had spoken to her.

At that moment, back aboard the tortured *Oregon*, Captain Williams heard a sound that strikes terror in the hearts of all seamen. He heard the awful roar of surf breaking upon a beach, and even though it came from downwind, the roar became louder and louder until it almost drowned out the scream of the wind.

Springing to his feet, Captain Williams put his face almost against the ear of the nearest helmsman and shouted at the top of his lungs, "Ease her off! Ease her off! There are breakers ahead. We'll have to beach her! It's our only chance!"

Nodding his head grimly, the sailor nudged his fellow-helmsman with an elbow, and together they strained to turn the ship's wheel until the *Oregon* was running, like a wild thing, dead before the wind with the towering seas racing at them from astern.

Oceanographers tell us that there is within each hurricane a phenomenon that they call "the surge." This is a giant monster of a wave that springs from the very heart of the storm and drives everything before it with such force that nothing can stand in its way. It is this "surge" that destroys millions of dollars worth of beach property and drowns many people and animals in its path. The surge was the giant wave that laid the offshore *Washington* over on her beam ends and washed away and drowned most of her crew. As it so happened, this was also the wave that came upon the *Oregon* from astern as she turned her bow toward the beach and made a run for the lives of her crew.

By now some of the cargo of the *Oregon* had shifted forward under the stress of the storm, and she was riding rather high in the water at the stern, much like a Chinese junk. The huge surge, sweeping all before it, came upon the *Oregon* and lifted her, like a large surfboard, and flung her on the leading edge of the surge up and completely over the barrier beach, the sand dunes, and the trees, dropping her with a thud on a sand shoal in the waters of the sound. At the same time, the surge cut a tremendous gash into the barrier beach and sluiced out thousands of cubic yards of sand into the water behind the barrier reef, piling millions of gallons of sea water up into the sound. Within an hour, the demon wind had shifted all the way around to the southwest. Back came that great mound of water, back through the gap already cut by the storm, dredging it deeper and deeper, until a genuine inlet was cut that very night. Hatteras Inlet was created that same night by that same awful hurricane and has remained open ever since. The *Oregon* remained stuck on her sandbar inside the new inlet until two days later, when the wind and water had subsided enough for her cargo to be jettisoned. Thus lightened, she floated free.

There are other stories about the naming of Oregon Inlet. One respected historian and researcher has painted a beautiful word-picture of a steamboat named *Oregon* paddlewheeling serenely through the inlet, the first ship to pass through after the inlet had been gouged out and the sea had returned to a glassy calm. Most of the old-timers, however, believe that it was Captain Williams' *Oregon* that was hurled through as the inlet was being born and thus lent her name to the new passageway through the barrier. Mr. Edward R. Outlaw, Jr., was one of the earliest visitors to this portion of the Outer Banks, and his family's oceanfront cottage—still standing and very much in use—was one of the first built in the area. In his wonderful book, *Old Nag's Head*, Mr. Outlaw tells of Captain Williams, whom he knew personally, relating this story to him when the captain was seventy-five or eighty years old.

Since it was born in September of 1846, Oregon Inlet has "migrated" some three and one-half to four miles southward, as is shown on the following sketches from maps of the U.S. Coastal Survey. The later map clearly shows the sand shoal (which later grew into an island) on which *Oregon* fetched up after her wild ride.

Now, you may choose to call it blind luck that the schooner rode the surge through the inlet as it was being created by the storm, but you couldn't have convinced Miss Penelope Williams of that. She knew in her heart of hearts that her dear mother had come back from the grave to warn her of her brother's peril. The Almighty Himself had strengthened her in her conviction that God does, indeed, intervene in the affairs of men and that "the prayers of the righteous availeth much."

Personally, I'm with Miss Penelope.

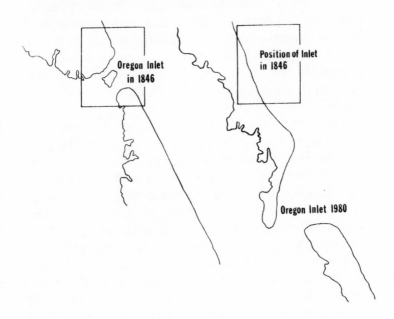

TEA PARTIES
AND PATRIOTS

*B*ACK IN 1773, the British colonies on the Atlantic Seaboard of this country were in turmoil. The British government persisted in treating their American cousins more like a foreign country than like colonies of their own kin. Resentment ran high.

In those days there were many bonds between Edenton, the town named for the royal governor of North Carolina, and Boston in the colony of Massachusetts. Both were ports of entry and important trading centers in the new world. Commerce between them grew and prospered. Not only that, but many of the families intermarried so that there were blood cousins in both places.

Thus, when some of the young men of Boston disguised themselves as Indians and raided three English ships in Boston harbor, throwing overboard their cargoes of chests of tea, the people of Edenton applauded. This famous Boston Tea Party occurred on December 16, 1773, and was a dramatic protest against the infamous Tea Act by which the British sought greatly to increase the cost of the Americans' favorite beverage.

When the British promptly closed the Boston harbor after the Tea Party, Bostonians found themselves in dire need of foodstuffs and other necessities. They would have fared badly had not the Edentonians dispatched ships, notably the vessel *Penelope*, laden with food and other relief supplies.

As matters worsened with England, the ladies of Edenton thought it high time that they took a stand and showed the world their support of their menfolk.

And so it came about that on October 25, 1774, fifty-one matrons met at the home of Mrs. Elizabeth King near the courthouse commons and there foreswore the further use of English tea, theretofore their favorite beverage and delightful social adjunct. To emphasize their stand, they poured their tea on the ground and emptied their tea caddies. In addition to Mrs. King, these patriots included Mrs. Penelope Barker, president of the meeting, Abigail Charlton, Elizabeth Creacy, Anne Johnston, Sarah Littlejohn, Jean Blair, Anne Horniblow, and others.

They actually wrote down their declaration, and after setting out their admiration and support of the position of the Carolina men, they concluded, "We the Ladys of Edenton do hereby solemnly engage not to conform to that pernicious practice of drinking tea, or that we the aforesaid Ladys will not permit ye wear of any manufacture from England, until such time that all acts which tend to enslave this our native country shall be repealed." Each of the ladies then signed the declaration. It was made part of the official record, and copies were sent to England. The women of North Carolina had spoken out bravely in support of their men and of their sister city to the north.

As relations with the mother country grew worse and worse, North Carolinians began to talk openly of rebellion. The famous Halifax Resolves were to put the

Tar Heel State in the very forefront of the growing movement for open rebellion against the mother country. The spirit of the Magna Carta burned in the breasts of these expatriated Englishmen as fiercely as it ever had in Britons. It is remarkable that the king's counselors did not recognize this spirit. Instead, they blundered on with their heavy-handed policy of rule or ruin. With the exception of such farsighted statesmen as William Pitt the Younger, England thus pushed America toward the brink of war.

Living in Edenton at that time was an Englishman by the name of Joseph Hewes who had settled there a decade before and developed a large and profitable maritime trade. He built many of the wharves that served the port, and he owned a number of sailing vessels with which he carried on an extensive trade both at home and abroad. This same Joseph Hewes was later to become one of North Carolina's signers of the Declaration of Independence.

Also in Edenton was a young seaman named John Paul Jones. In spite of his youth, he was a capable captain, and it is thought that he commanded many of Hewes' vessels on trips to Ocracoke and Portsmouth Island, as well as to the West Indies. There was much coming and going between Edenton and North Carolina's Outer Banks even in those days.

When war finally came, young John Paul Jones applied for a commission in the fighting ships of the colonists. There were two problems with his application. In the first place, it was thought that he did not have the experience or the skill for such an important position. In the second, the colonists had no navy, as such, with which to fight the British fleet—at that time the strongest in the world. Observing these problems, Jones' friend and erstwhile employer came to the aid of both his protégé and his country.

Incredible as it may seem, Joseph Hewes made a gift of all his ships to his country and thus helped to form the nucleus of the Yankee fleet. It is said that this magnanimous gesture, coupled with urgings from Hewes, persuaded the Continental Congress to name young John Paul Jones as a first lieutenant of the Continental Navy. History has proved the wisdom of this decision. The young lieutenant became what one historian has called "the greatest fighting naval commander America ever had." His spirited "Sir, I've not yet begun to fight" is one of the proudest traditions of the United States Navy.

The war for freedom was fought and won, and the story of the Edenton patriots might have had a completely happy ending, but tradition has added one poignant note.

Also living in Edenton at the time of the Revolution was a family who shall remain nameless here, except to say that the lady of the house was one of the fifty-one celebrants at the tea party. She had a lovely daughter who was in her teens, and their home was one of the most beautiful in the entire town. It had a large and gracious front porch and a second story porch, both of which ran the entire length of the house. This fine home was located on a street that ran down to Queen Anne's Creek and is designated on present-day maps of Edenton as Oakum Street.

The young girl was very much in love with a sailor

and he with her. He was also very patriotic, and like Jones, he volunteered his services and his skill as a seaman to his fledgling country.

It is said that after her lover sailed away to fight for the colonies, the young girl and her mother spent many long hours rolling bandages and making uniforms for the soldiers and sailors who were fighting the British. Although in those days it might have been considered slightly immodest, she also knitted socks for her sailor and had them sent to him. Day and night she prayed for his safety and his return. She read the casualty lists with great dread, but the name of her beloved never appeared on any catalogue of those killed or lost at sea.

When Cornwallis finally surrendered at Yorktown, the town of Edenton went wild with joy. There were celebrations and bonfires, and the returning servicemen were greeted with great pride.

Day after long day the young girl waited for her sailor's return. She would pace up and down the length of that upper balcony, calling out to her lover, at first softly and then more and more loudly, "O come back, my lover! O come back to me! O come! O come!"

Finally, they say, she lost her mind and went completely mad. Until she died, she would walk that balcony night after night, crying out in a loud, clear voice, "O come! O come! O come!" until all the neighbors wept for pity.

The older residents will tell you that the street now called "Oakum Street" was for years and years correctly called "O Come Street" in memory of the young girl whose lover never returned.

If one of them tells you this, please don't laugh. Many of them believe it to be the very truth. Long before the street signs were erected, the story was told to them as fact.

For my part, I think I prefer the spelling in the legend to the spelling on the present-day town map.

THE LEGEND OF
BATTS' GRAVE

*S*OME MEN seem born to be pioneers and frontiersmen. Men like Daniel Boone and Davy Crockett seem, somehow, to loom larger than life. The stories of their lives and exploits read like fictional tales of high adventures that are somehow far beyond the abililties and the opportunities of most men.

Such a man was an Englishman named Jesse Batts (or Batz). The tales and legends about him seem to be based upon hard, historical fact.

Batts came over from England to this country in advance of most of the settlers and farmers and apparently lived an idyllic life as a trader — a woodsman, hunter, and fisherman par excellence.

In 1653 young Batts was commissioned by Sir Francis Yardley to explore to the south of Jamestown to see if he could find any trace of Sir Walter Raleigh's "Lost Colony." It was on this trip that Batts discovered Caratoke (Currituck) Inlet and proceeded to "Rhoanok" Island, where he made friends with the Indians and was shown the ruins of Sir Walter Raleigh's fort.

Batts got along well with the great men and captains of the Indians and spent several weeks persuading them to "come and make peace with the English." When he returned to Sir Francis' settlement in Virginia, Batts was well received and honored not only for his discovery of the inlet, but also for his part in making peace with the Indians.

Official documents establish that on May 25, 1656, he married Mary Woodhouse, who was the widow and second wife of a Colonel Woodhouse and was a lady of some wealth and position.

Jesse was apparently not a very good businessman, for he soon ran into trouble with his creditors. The records of the quarter court of "James City" reveal that in 1657 the court took official note of the great pains and trouble Batts had gone through in the discovery of the inlet and for that reason ordered that he be protected from his creditors for a period of one year. Nothing whatsoever was said in the judgment about his services as peacemaker to the Indians.

Soon thereafter our hero became estranged from his rich wife, and fed up with the toils of "civilization," he set forth on a journey into the wilds to the south, where he had been so well received by the natives.

Batts made his home on the island that still bears his name on the upper reaches of the Albemarle Sound, just about one mile east from what is now known as Drummond's Point and about one-half mile south of the present Harvey's Neck, where the Yeopim River and Yeopim Creek merge and flow into the broad waters of the sound. This is several miles southwest across the waters of the sound from Durant's Neck, where some of the very earliest settlements in North Carolina were later to be made. On present-day charts of the United

States Coast and Geodetic Survey (C & G Chart No. 1228), this little speck of land is still identified as "Batz' Grave," and thereby hangs this tale.

In those days, the waters of the sounds, creeks, and rivers teemed with fish of many kinds, and the forests abounded with herds of deer and bison and multitudes of rabbits, raccoons, gray foxes, bears, cougars or panthers, and other game. This paradise was home to several tribes of Indians and to just one white man, Jesse Batts.

As we have seen, our young frontiersman was on quite good terms with the Algonquins, who inhabited and hunted over all the area that was later to become northeastern North Carolina. He was especially familiar with the tribe called Chowanoc (the name means "Southerners" or "Men to the South"). Their principal town of Chepanoc was just a short distance by water from the island home of Batts, and he visited the town often, sometimes staying weeks at a time. The Chowanocs frequently visited his island, which they called Kalola or "Island of Many Gulls."

The King of the Chowanocs, old Kilkanoo, took a special liking to the Englishman and saw to it that he was taught much Indian lore. For example, the young man was shown how the natives made their dugout canoes. First a cypress of suitable size was felled by constant application of fire around its base. After the top was removed by similar burning, the log was hoisted upon a sort of stand made of forked posts, and the boat was formed by burning out the interior and scraping out the charred wood. Eventually a trough was formed, which was further burned and scraped into a serviceable boat. Some of these craft were large enough to carry twenty men, while others were created to carry only one or two persons. They were serviceable enough for crossing the broad rivers and sounds of the country, but they were quite "tippy" or unstable, and a good sense of balance was required to keep them upright, particularly in any kind of wind.

Jesse was also introduced to the cultivation and harvest of the white potato. Although it is mistakenly called the "Irish potato" down to this very day, this nourishing tuber originated with the Indians of coastal Carolina and Virginia and was carried back to England by homing explorers. There it soon became a dietary staple, not only of the Irish, but of other Europeans as well.

All this he learned, plus the skills of chasing down the black bear with "much whooping and hollering," the cornering of bison and deer when they wandered into deep woods, the spearing of fish, and the construction of weirs in the sounds to trap some of the millions of herring when they migrated westward on their spawning runs. And so Jesse Batts lived the life of an Indian brave and practiced their ways.

King Kilkanoo had an only child, a daughter named Kickawanna, who was the joy and the light of his life. A few years younger than Jesse Batts, she was possessed of a rare, wild beauty that soon won the heart of the young Englishman. Lithe and active, she went about unashamedly naked except for the traditional apron of the Indian women and, occasionally, a copper breastplate bearing her father's royal insignia. Her skin was a light gold in color, and her laughing eyes and keen intelligence had made her a favorite with all the tribe. Many young braves had courted her and had petitioned her father for her hand, but she had eyes only for the young frontiersman, and Kilkanoo was determined that she should have a mate of her own choosing and not be forced into a union. She liked her young Chowanoc contemporaries well enough and was friendly with them, but she much preferred the company of young Batts. Besides, the braves smelled too much of rancid bear grease, which they used as an insect repellent, and they could not tell her wonderful tales of the land beyond the great sea and the marvels of the white man's world.

They roamed the woods together, the Englishman and his Indian princess. They were as happy as children, fishing and swimming and making love and reveling in the nectar of their youth in a land brimming with beauty and with food aplenty for the taking in a mild and salubrious climate. It was, indeed, a Garden of Eden before the advent of the serpent.

And that serpent was not long in making an appearance.

To the north and east of the hunting grounds of the Chowanocs lay the territory claimed and used by another Algonquian tribe called the Paspatank, whose king was Chief Pamunky.

Both tribes used the territory separating their towns as a common hunting ground. On a hunting expedition through that ground toward Kilkanoo's town of Chepanoc, Pamunky was creeping silently through the woods, taking care to make as little noise as possible in the hope of coming upon an unsuspecting deer or bear.

As he stopped and listened for telltale sounds of a possible quarry, Pamunky heard the sound of water splashing off to his right. His eyes gleamed with anticipation as he turned in that direction. He believed that he had come upon a beaver pond, which would furnish him with many valuable pelts to use in trade with other tribes.

As he approached, the splashing grew louder, and he silently parted the bushes. There he beheld, not a colony of beavers, but the beautiful Kickawanna bathing in the waters of Yeopim Creek.

He knew not who she was, but he knew that he had to have this beautiful thing as his own. With a savage cry, he burst from the bushes and began to slog through the water toward the frightened girl, who was quite alone. With muscular arms outstretched and an evil grin on his lips, Pamunky lunged toward the maid who was scrambling with all her might to climb out on the opposite bank and escape.

She reached the bank just seconds before her attacker and, grabbing up her apron with one hand, she wheeled and picked up her copper breastplate with the other.

Like a vampire confronted with a cross, her attacker fell back and stared with awe and respect at the breastplate. Copper itself denoted royalty to him, and he well knew the crest of his neighboring chief, Kilkanoo. He also knew the fate that would probably befall him, king or not, if he harmed the girl. Taken completely aback, the hunting chief turned and silently made his way back to his own town of Pasquenoke.

The next day King Pamunky called a meeting of his entire tribal council, with his medicine men and his captains and his senior advisors, and asked for their advice in his desire to have the lovely Princess Kickawanna as his squaw. The king had had many concubines, but no wife according to the laws of the Algonquin. He needed a son and heir to lead the children of his tribesmen. This potential union with Kickawanna, then, was of extreme importance, and the great council deliberated long and performed many rituals.

After much talk and invocation of the spirits, including dances and the burning of uppowoc (tobacco) as a sacrifice to the evil spirits, the council at last gave the chief its decision.

"Oh, great King," said the chief shaman or medicine man, "we believe a good spirit has brought this about for the benefit of our tribe. Let us go to our blood brothers, the Chowanocs, and sit in solemn council with them to propose that this beautiful princess be given as wife to you, and that thus our two tribes shall be united as one upon the death of old King Kilkanoo. This union will greatly strengthen our tribe and double the number of our fighting men. Thus will the Paspatank become the greatest tribe in the land."

And so it came to pass that a messenger was sent to the Chowanocs with a proposal for a joint council meeting to take place several weeks thence, on the Moon of the Corn, to discuss "certain matters of great portent to both the tribes."

Now, Princess Kickawanna had not told her father of the encounter with Pamunky in the forest, and even had she done so, it is unlikely the Chowanocs could have divined the true purpose of the conference. The Paspatank messenger was sent on his way back to his people laden with many gifts and with the Chowanoc acceptance of the proposed meeting in Chepanoc.

In Chepanoc, preparations for the great feast went forward with speed. The houses were cleaned and refurbished, and the women prepared a stew of corn, venison, and peas mixed with chunks of fish and shellfish, simmering it upon a slow fire to reach its peak of flavor on the Corn Moon. Jesse Batts, meanwhile, was away in his sloop trading with the Siouan tribes to the south and knew nothing of this impending great council.

On the day of the great event, King Pamunky arrived with twenty or more of his councilmen and captains, all of whom were dressed in their finest regalia and burdened down with ornaments and decorations of paint and dyes upon various parts of their bodies.

Language was no barrier since both tribes were Algonquian, nor were customs or protocol any impediment as each worshipped the same gods, feared the same evil spirits, and had similar traditions.

After much feasting and dancing and smoking of tobacco, the purpose of the Paspatanks was explained with much imagery and eloquent statement of the advantages to be realized if the proposal were accepted.

King Kilkanoo listened with courtesy and heard the visitors out in full. Then he promised a decision on the morrow, saying that he wished first to consult his daughter, Princess Kickawanna. The Paspatanks were astonished by the king's words. It was almost unheard of at that time to consider the opinion of the woman involved in such a question. Nevertheless, the tribe had to respect the king's wishes.

On the next day, as promised, King Kilkanoo gave the visitors his answer. In as courteous and diplomatic terms as he could command, he declined the offer and explained that the reason behind his decision was the simple fact that his daughter preferred another.

Pamunky was furious. At the risk of his own life, he stood up in council and called the host king everything but honorable, accusing him of being a weak and senile old man who would put the wishes of a mere squaw ahead of the welfare of his people.

Growing more angry and reckless as he spoke, the visitor then vowed that what had been denied him by treaty, he would take by force. He swore that he would personally see to it that King Kilkanoo was slain at the same time. He even gave the date and the time when he would return to carry out his threats: on the first day of the first Moon of the Cohonks (named after the cries of the wild goose, which returned about that time each year).

This setting of a time and place for a fixed battle was rare, too, among the Indian tribes, but legend insists that this is what happened. At the appointed time and location, Pamunky returned with his warriors and attacked Chepanoc.

Jesse Batts had returned to his Island of Many Gulls and to the palisaded town of Chepanoc two days after Pamunky had stormed out of the great council. The trader was appalled at the trouble and danger his love for his Indian maid had caused his dark-skinned friends. He lost no time in telling his love how deeply he was touched by their loyalty and steadfastness, and he asked to be heard in council.

Although it was unusual for a white man to be heard in council, the members granted his request. He pleaded so sincerely to be allowed to help in the upcoming war that the elders and captains agreed that he should become a member of the tribe and should be allowed to fight alongside them in the pending battle.

With more singing and dancing by the costumed medicine men and much throwing of tobacco and sand in the air to appease any evil spirits, the Chowanocs went through the ceremony making Batts a full-fledged Algonquian brave. Using the sharpened edge of an enormous oyster shell, the shaman cut a small incision on the inner forearm of the initiate and cut one on his own arm. Then the other priests bound the arms together with rawhide so that the two wounds were pressed together. The blood of the white man mixed with the blood of the holy Indian man and dripped in great, red drops to the ground.

Batts had been accepted as blood-brother with the Chowanocs.

As the time for the prearranged battle drew near, Jesse tried to make himself as much an Indian in appearance as he was now in law. He refused to crop his luxuriant blond beard, but he trimmed his hair Indian-style with a topknot and feathers and painted a large red circle around one eye and an equally large white one around the other. On Batts' left shoulder blade, the medicine men dyed the insignia of the Chowanocs, three parallel arrows of different lengths, each tipped with the spur of a wild grouse and fledged with feathers of the wild turkey. They presented him with a huge Indian war club, fashioned out of a lightwood knot and baked for hours until it had become almost as hard as iron.

At the appointed hour, the warriors of the Paspatanks attacked. Scores of them slipped from the woods surrounding the clearing around the Chowanoc town and unleashed flight after flight of fire arrows. Arcing over the palisades, the moss-tipped flaming missiles came down upon the straw and dry-reed roofs of the houses and started several fires. The Chowanocs were not taken by surprise. The veteran warriors of the tribe had warned of this tactic, and the women and young boys were ready with gourds and wooden buckets of water to throw on the flames and with green boughs from the hardwood forest to beat out the fire.

Failing to create panic among the defenders, the beseiging force tried a frontal attack on the palisades to force an entrance but were driven back by cloud after cloud of war arrows from inside the town.

As the invaders fell back to regroup, the men of Chowanoc came screaming and leaping out of their town in counterattack.

For hours the battle raged in the clearing and in the adjacent woods. Casualties were many. King Kilkanoo was struck in the shoulder by one of the flaming arrows and fell to the ground, seriously wounded.

Jesse Batts dodged and danced through the melee until he was able to locate King Pamunky standing tall and fierce with his huge muscles bulging under his war paint. Brandishing a wicked war club as he screamed epithets at the enemy, Pamunky cried out for revenge on King Kilkanoo.

Batts shouted one word: "Pamunky!" As the fierce

warrior turned toward him, the two joined in eye-gouging, groin-kicking, cutting, and slashing conflict. The trader disdained the use of a gun and carried only his hatchet and his hunting knife into battle along with the war club appended to his breechclout. The blood flowed freely and matted with dust, and soon it would have been impossible to tell one combatant from the other had it not been for the golden beard of the Englishman gleaming like a banner in the late afternoon sun.

Eventually the young trader prevailed. Several stout whacks alongside Pamunky's head with the war club finally rendered the chief almost senseless and he fell to his knees. As he was reaching again for his knife, a solid kick under the chin sent the invading chief sprawling flat on his back. Batts moved in for the kill, war club raised and foot planted firmly upon his enemy's throat.

Sensing his own immediate demise, Pamunky, in decidedly unchiefly terror, began to scream and pray for mercy, promising anything—anything at all—if only his life were spared. His warriors near him stared in slack-jawed disbelief.

All of this would have done the defeated man absolutely no good had not the lovely Princess Kickawanna come rushing at that moment from the shelter of the palisade. Racing up to her lover, she placed her hand upon his upraised arm and begged for the life of her enemy, pleading that enough blood had already been shed.

Batts relented and lowered his club, but before he would allow Pamunky and his surviving warriors to go, he asked that King Kilkanoo be summoned from the town. With the shaft of the Paspatank arrow still protruding from his shoulder, the old king demonstrated one of the reasons he was so respected as chief. He agreed to spare Pamunky and to forego the custom of making the defeated braves become slaves to the Chowanocs, but only in return for the solemn promise by the defeated chief and his surviving captains that they would never again set foot upon the territory of the Chowanocs in peace or in war, and that they would deed one-half of the Paspatank territory to the Chowanocs. The Paspatank tribesmen immediately presented to the victors a rather large clod of earth, held together by the grass growing out of it, to symbolize the transfer of exclusive rights to the ceded territory. This done, the Paspatanks took their dead and their wounded and disappeared into the woods, never again to trouble the Chowanocs.

We can imagine the victory celebrations that took place in the town of Chepanoc. Long and loud were the praises of King Kilkanoo and of the new Indian, Jesse Batts. The old king in time recovered from the arrow wound in his shoulder, as did Batts from the many knife wounds he had received.

By unanimous vote of the tribal council, Batts was named a prince of the tribe, second in rank only to the king. His and Kickawanna's request that they be allowed to marry in the beautiful traditional ceremony of the Algonquian royalty was granted.

By custom, at least two moons had to elapse from the time of the granting of the decree of engagement until the ceremony itself. The days and nights of waiting were ones of complete happiness for the young couple. For privacy they spent most of their evenings on Batts'

Island of Many Gulls. Princess Kickawanna would paddle her small dugout canoe over the bright waters to the
island, a trip of several miles there and back to her
father's town.

Whether the high priests had failed to appease one of
the evil spirits they dreaded so much, or whether it was
just the intervention of fate, the wedding was not to be.

One night, as Princess Kickawanna paddled her frail
canoe over the broad waters of the Albemarle Sound
toward her lover's island, a terrible line squall developed. The face of the moon was suddenly hidden by a
line of black thunderheads driving across the sky. The
wind rose to gale force and the placid waters of the
sound were whipped into large, breaking waves.

The princess was never seen again, although Batts
and his Indian friends searched for days on end along
the shores of the sound. Her disappearance was complete. Neither her little canoe nor her body was ever
found.

Jesse Batts sank into a slough of despair. His sloop lay
unattended at his pier and gradually sank to the bottom,
still tied to a piling. His fish weirs went unattended and
his garden grew up in weeds. The Chowanocs visited
him regularly and tried to cheer him, but to no avail.
Although he would occasionally eat a small amount of
the food with which they sought to tempt him, he
gradually grew weaker. He would not leave his island.

One day his friends found him dead in the little house
he had built for his bride. There on his island, they gave
him a white man's burial, even placing a rude cross in
the form of sticks tied together at his grave. From that
day to this, the little island that the Indians called

"Island of Many Gulls" has been known simply as Batts' Grave.

The Albemarle Sound near Batts' Grave still abounds in fish and other marine life and is fished regularly by commercial and sport fishermen and crabbers and oystermen. If you can gain their confidence, there are many oldsters among them who will swear to you with a straight face and complete sincerity that on the nights of the full moon that the Indians called the Moon of the Corn, and the first and second Moons of the Cohonks, if you will go very quietly to a spot offshore from Batts' Grave, you can clearly see him wandering up and down the strand. His blond beard, they say, still waves in the breeze, and you can hear him pitifully calling out to his lost bride, "Kickawanna...Kickawanna...come back...come back...come back."

THE TALE OF
THE SEA HORSE

*T*HE SEA HORSE is an interesting little ocean creature. Although it thrives all along North Carolina's Outer Banks, you may surf and fish and swim there many times and never see one unless you are observant. Not much bigger than a man's finger, it is not very conspicuous in its saltwater environment.

Ichthyologists will tell you that the sea horse belongs to the genus *Hippocamus*. These scientists may further tell you that the creature is related to the prehistoric coelacanth, which until a few years ago was thought to be long extinct. The sea horse has a prehensile tail with which it grasps seaweed, and instead of scales, it has armor-like plates of bone, which protect the creature and form its outer skin. With the exception of its tail and its bony armor, it looks almost exactly like a minature horse.

All of these things and more these students of matters piscatorial can tell you, but they cannot tell you why.

There was a Scot named Angus McAngus who knew —or at least claimed to know—the answer to that primordial why and how.

Angus was a true Scotsman who hailed from the shores of northern Scotland, and he had followed the sea all of his life. He had sailed mostly on whaling ships and had been so badly injured in so many battles with the leviathan of the deep that he could no longer follow the sea and do a seaman's work. He had migrated to this country and had settled in the almost legendary Diamond City on the Outer Banks in what is now Carteret County. There he took what part he could in the shore base of a whaling operation. He would help cut up the blubber from the whales that were brought ashore and would tend the giant metal vats in which it was rendered. Angus was shore-bound for the rest of his life and he hated it. But there were compensations.

Sometimes the ancient Scot would regale the children of Diamond City with his salty tales of the sea and seafaring men, as well as the legends of the ocean deeps. One of their favorites was his tale of the sea horse.

Before telling a story, Angus would make himself comfortable in the beach sand near a huge bonfire and take several long pulls from the square bottle he always kept handy to ward off sea snakes. "Aye, my wee bairnes," he would say, "ol' Angus kens the tale o' the mickle sea horse. 'Tis a Scottish tale and comes from the shores o' the the North Sea in my homeland. 'Tis an auld , auld tale. Back in the days of auld lang syne things were muckle happier than they be today." With his rich burr adding to the charm of the story, he would then tell the assembled starry-eyed children the much-loved story of the "mickle" sea horse.

According to Angus, when the world and the sea were first made there was much sport and camaraderie among the creatures of the deep. The ancestors of the present-day sea horses were huge creatures then, big as any Arabian thoroughbred and just as fast and frisky. They were half fish and half horse, and the kings of the undersea world rode them and raced them, one against another. They were never used as work horses, although the rulers of the ocean enjoyed riding them for great distances when they had a journey to make. There were even racing meets at which the sea horses would be pitted against each other in a sort of elimination tournament until a champion of the meet would be chosen. They say that some of the other sea creatures would place bets of pearls and diamonds and other precious jewels on a favorite horse.

After awhile, though, trouble raised its ugly head.

On the coasts of Scotland, particularly the North Sea Coast, there appeared a terrible creature the Scots called the Kelpie. This Kelpie was a wild gray horse who roamed the beach looking for children he could abduct. He was an evil spirit in horse form, and like most evil spirits, he was almost fatally charming and appealing. He had a velvety coat and soft green eyes. Long eyelashes lent a misleading aura of gentleness, and children were charmed when he would canter up. They would rub his smooth coat and look into his beautiful green eyes, and some of them would even climb aboard for a horseback ride.

This was always a grevious mistake. Once astride the Kelpie, the children found they were stuck fast and could not dismount. Try as they would, they were securely fastened to its back. With a toss of its head the beast would then gallop into the sea and, once offshore, would dive down to the bottom of the sea, carrying the children with him to their fate.

Once it had them in its power, the Kelpie would then change them into strange enchanted creatures that the Scots called Selkies or man-seals. They would be both land and sea creatures then, taking the form of a seal when they were in the water and of a human when they were ashore. It was their unhappy fate to be forever dissatisfied whether they were in the sea or on land, for they would forever long for the other element. Their sea-longing would turn to land-longing and their land-longing would become sea-longing so that they were miserable for the rest of their lives.

The Scots hunted the Kelpie but were never able to capture or to harm it. Their most powerful magicians were not able to help. In their extremity, they turned to Poseidon, god of the deep waters, earthquakes, and horses, and brother of the great Zeus himself. They told this sea king what was happening and begged his help lest all their children be turned into Selkies.

Poseidon was very angry and agreed to help. He immediately began an undersea search for this creature so that he could be bound and imprisoned beneath the sea, but search as he would, he could find nothing about the whereabouts of the dread Kelpie. The reason was that the sea horses were hiding him in the mistaken belief that he was their kin. They could not believe that any horse could be so evil, and so they hid him, for a long time thwarting the sea king's effort to bring him to justice.

Finally, however, a wise old loggerhead turtle told Poseidon where the sea horses were hiding the Kelpie, and the ruler of the deep was able to corner the monster and chain him forever in a cave in the bottom of the North Sea so that never again could he harm the children of the Scots.

Understandably very angry with the sea horses for

their part in hiding the Kelpie, Poseidon put them on trial for their offenses. They were, in time, found guilty of obstructing sea-justice and given a severe punishment.

From that day on, Poseidon declared, the sea horses were to be changed from large, fast racers into tiny little creatures no longer than a finger. Instead of being the companions of the sea gods, they were from thenceforth to be the work horses of the millions of tiny sea elves who lived on the ocean floor and tended the crops of seaweed. These tiny elves would harness them and plow with them and use them for beasts of burden. The sea horses would still enjoy many of the pleasures of the deep, but always their worlds and their pleasures would be in minature. They would be protected from predatory fishes by strong armor, and they would multiply and have many children, but never, except in memory, would they enjoy their former position of importance in the kingdom of the undersea.

As he finished his story, Angus would almost always fall into a deep sleep while the beach fire slowly faded and died into glowing coals. Almost always the children would tug at his sleeve and beg for another story before they had to go to bed. All they could ever get was a snort and a resonant snore as the old whaler wriggled into a more comfortable postion in the warm sand and committed himself to pleasant dreams of the sea.

A DISMAL SWAMP
LOVE STORY

*T*HE GREAT DISMAL SWAMP of North Carolina and Virginia is a natural wonder and, in some respects, a contradiction. It lies athwart the Carolina–Virginia line and is about equal in area in each state. Covering a total of nearly one thousand square miles, it is blessed with copious rainfall and the flora and fauna are abundant, to say the least. Ferns grow taller than a man's head, and even down to the present day, large populations of deer, bear, raccoons, opossums, bobcats, rabbits, and squirrels abound. It is both the northernmost habitat for numerous subtropical plants and animals, and the southernmost locale for another large group that is classified as being northern in occurrence.

Snakes there grow to be huge. Since these reptiles apparently continue to grow as long as they live, and since they have few natural enemies in the swamp, it is not at all unusual to encounter specimens as large around as a man's thigh.

Parts of the swamp are huge beds of quicksand. Other parts quake under a person's feet as though the whole surface were about to collapse.

It is, indeed, a fearsome and a beautiful place.

In the center of this wilderness is a large lake named Lake Drummond. Strangely, the water of this lake is not stagnant at all but is extremely acid and is even used to preserve game. Even more strange, the surface water of the region does not drain into the central lake. On the contrary, the lake water drains outward, and no fewer than seven rivers or streams flow therefrom in all directions. One of these streams is the Blackwater River, and it flows into North Carolina's Currituck Sound.

For years man has tried to tame the Great Dismal, but without very much success. In the early days of our country, George Washington became much interested in the area and was one of several men who tried unsuccessfully to drain the swamp for reclamation. Some canals were cut and the flow of the water outward from the swamp was speeded somewhat, but that was about the extent of the venture.

It is said that the father of our country was surveying in the swamp on one occasion when he happened to confront a large black bear on a narrow trail. Not being used to humans and being unafraid of them, the bear was not inclined to retreat, and General Washington feared that if he himself fled, he would encourage pursuit. To one side of the narrow path was quicksand, and to the other an amber-colored stream containing several large snakes.

Displaying the tactical genius that distinguished him on the battlefield, the founding father is said to have climbed a nearby tree, and the bear ambled past and on down the path until he was out of sight. Elated at eluding the bear, the father of our nation was hastening to descend when he slipped and fell into the water, scattering surprised moccasins in all directions. To his own surprise, Washington found the water to be very deep. Never did his feet touch bottom before the natural buoyancy of his body brought him again to the surface. From that day until this, the location where this is said to have happened has been called Deep Creek. It is now a thriving community, but in those days, it was almost the heart of the wilderness.

The early Indian tribes knew the Dismal, and in a later day, runaway slaves found the fens a natural hiding place from pursuit. Being such a horrible, fascinating, and dangerous place, it was inevitable that fables and legends about it should grow like the luxurious foliage found there.

One of these legends, which has been told and retold for generations, is the subject of this story. It concerns the Indians who once lived and hunted on the borders of the Dismal; the undying love of a man for a maid; and the unfathomable ways of the Great Spirit.

Long before the white man came to these shores, the native Indian tribes lived and flourished in the wonderfully temperate climate. The abundance of game and the rich fertility of the soil made it ideal for their way of life. They took from the land and from the forests only what they needed to sustain life, and the various tribes were generally at peace with one another. Most of the tribes were Algonquian, and they formed into several confederacies, notably the Weapemeoc confederacy in what is now the Albemarle region of North Carolina and the Chesapeoc confederacy of tribes in what is now southeastern Virginia.

It was the custom of the chiefs of these confederacies to exchange sons when the braves were quite young, so that they would grow up in the family of a neighboring chief and thus bind the confederacies even closer together. This exchange usually worked quite well. While the young men did not forget their natural parents and the elders of their home tribe, they grew accustomed to the viewpoints and needs of their adopted group and served as a sort of bridge to promote good feeling.

Running Deer was the name the Chesapeocs gave to the young prince the Weapemeocs sent to live and grow up with them, and the host chief grew as fond of him as he was of his own sons. Also very fond of him was the daughter of the household, a beautiful young maid called Moon Flower.

As these two grew from childhood into adulthood together, their life developed into an idyllic love story. Running Deer became a great hunter and fisherman who was noted for his bravery and his wisdom, and Moon Flower became more beautiful and more kind and loving as she matured.

The two lovers roamed the forests and streams together. They loved best of all to paddle their canoe on the waters of what is now Lake Drummond, but which the Indians called The Lake of a Thousand Ghosts. Their very favorite place was located on the far side of the lake from their village. It was a small island on which grew a tremendous cypress tree. Indians called the island a dwelling place of the Great Spirit. There Moon Flower and Running Deer would kneel in the white sand before the tree and pour out to the Great Spirit their dreams and plans. They told how they wanted to be married and to have papooses of their own and to raise them to revere the Great Spirit and all his creations.

Finally, late one summer in the first Moon of the Wild Goose, they told Moon Flower's father of their plans and wishes. The old chief was not at all surprised, for he had not been blind to the attachment that had grown up between them. To say he was delighted would be an understatement. He was overjoyed at the prospect of having this splendid young brave bound to his family by yet another tie.

He agreed with Running Deer that the young man should journey back to his real father and receive a paternal blessing on the union; then he would return for the week-long marriage festivities.

Moon Flower was vaguely disturbed about the proposed journey. The way was long, and she very much wanted to go with Running Deer, but to do so was forbidden. He must go alone to his native tribe and alone must seek the approval of his father-chief before returning for the marriage. The betrothal could not even be sanctioned before this journey was made, and Running Deer was understandably eager to get started on the long path that would lead back, he hoped, to his beloved. His travel would be through the hunting grounds of friendly tribes, so he felt he would be quite safe from attack. He took his hunting bows and his fishing tackle, as he expected to live off the country as he journeyed, although he also took a small supply of sun-dried fish and strips of venison in case the hunting was not good.

On a beautiful, sunlit morning he left his adopted village and launched his canoe into the waters of one of the creeks flowing south out of the Lake of a Thousand

Ghosts. On the shore, Moon Flower waved a tearful goodbye.

Downstream Running Deer went until he reached the waters of what was even then called the Blackwater River. For several days the weather held for him and the hunting and fishing were good. As the river widened, however, the weather began to worsen until, by the time he reached the broad waters of the Chowan, a full-fledged storm was blowing. Finally, the storm reached hurricane force and Running Deer was forced to abandon his travel and seek shelter on an island in the river.

He had never seen such a storm! The wind howled and screamed as though a thousand devils were after him. The usually calm river changed into a pounding surf that threatened to engulf the island. The flimsy lean-to he built for shelter was whisked away by a gust of wind, and his canoe was washed away by the ever-rising tide of waves.

Running Deer sought safety on the higher ground of the interior of the island, but just at that instant, a large pine tree was twisted in two by the gale and the trunk fell on the Indian, breaking one of his legs and pinning him to the ground.

He did not know how long he lay pinned there, completely helpless. Several days went by, and he would surely have died had not a hunting party of Chowanocs found him and ministered to his needs. They took him back to their village, but he was delirious from his long exposure and fought them when they attempted to fasten crude splints to his broken leg.

In time their primitive but effective medicines did

their work, and Running Deer was restored to health. His leg mended slowly, but at last he resumed his journey in a borrowed dugout canoe and came to his father at the Weapemeoc village.

The aging chieftain was happy to give his consent to the proposed arrangement and called a special meeting of the council of elders to announce the betrothal and approaching marriage. They, too, gave unanimous consent and wished the young bridegroom a long life and many healthy children. Then, as now, royal marriages involved a great deal of protocol and ceremony.

Finally, however, Running Deer was free to return to his betrothed, and he set out in a splendid dugout canoe hollowed from a seasoned juniper log, the gift of the elders as a wedding present.

Propelling his frail craft with all the energy his young body could muster, he proceeded out into the broad waters of the sound and up the mouth of the mighty Chowan. Starting early in the mornings and sometimes paddling until darkness had fallen, the eager young brave hardly paused to eat as he hastened toward his love. At long last he once again entered the waters of the Blackwater River and knew he was approaching the village of his adopted tribe.

Upon reaching his destination, he found the town strangely quiet. The old chief's house of saplings and reeds was draped in the black feathers of mourning, and the few braves who were about would not look him in the eye but hurried past with bowed backs and downcast eyes.

When Running Deer finally located the elderly man, the chief was sitting crosslegged in the ceremonial hut, his face daubed with dark paint, singing a funeral dirge.

After grasping the forearm of his visitor, the old man told Running Deer what had happened. A great storm had struck the village several days after he had left and many people were killed. Moon Flower was unhurt, but she felt sure the storm had killed her lover, too. As day had followed long day, she had become wan and sickly and finally had died in spite of all the efforts of the medicine men.

Before she died, she had told them she wanted to be buried, not in the usual Indian fashion, but in the waters of the lake as near as possible to the giant tree that had been their altar and their trysting place. Her wishes had been carried out, and her body had been immersed in the water as she had requested. The village was still in mourning and her father was desolate.

Running Deer would not believe it. He could not accept the idea that the Great Spirit would do this to them after all their plans and dreams. No, his beloved was alive and was there at the lake waiting for him. He would find her.

Half-crazed with grief, he ran from the ceremonial lodge and off into the swamp. Onward he went, wading up the branch known as the Stream of Bitter Waters and on to the kingdom of the serpents. Finding the king of the serpents, he asked for news of his beloved, but the huge snake only hissed and swung his head from side to side.

Pressing still deeper into the swamp, he crossed the Land of the Trembling Earth where the very ground quivered with his every step and threatened to swallow him up, but he found no trace of his Moon Flower.

Finally he came to the shore opposite the place of the Great Spirit, and holding onto a log for support, he paddled himself over to the island.

For many hours he importuned the Great Spirit to return his bride to him that he might live and realize his dream. So pitiful was his plight and so earnest his plea that the Great Spirit had compassion on him and showed him a way he could regain his love.

In the night sky above, the Great Spirit showed him the bright band of stars we now call the Milky Way. Many moons ago, the distraught brave was told, the Indians to the south had a large corn mill where they ground their corn for meal, and they had stored a great quantity of this meal as an offering for the Great Spirit. On several mornings when they came to the mill, they found great quantities of the meal to be missing, so that the pile was growing less rather than increasing. Resolving to find the thief, they hid in the reeds surrounding the corn mill. Just before daybreak, a huge dog came out of the reeds and began to eat great mouthfuls of the fine meal. Shouting and screaming, the Indians ran at the dog and threw stones and sticks at him. Frightened, the great dog sprang into the sky and ran across the heavens, spilling a trail of cornmeal behind him. From that day, said the Great Spirit, the Indians have called this trail in the sky, "Where the Dog Ran." (Indeed, that is the Indian name for the Milky Way down to this day.)

The Great Spirit explained that Running Deer must now find the dog, tame him, and bring him back to help the Indians in the hunt. It was believed that the dog was hiding somewhere around the Lake of a Thousand Ghosts, but he was very cunning and would be hard to capture. To help in the search, Running Deer would be given the ghost of his beloved. If they succeeded in their task, they would both be allowed to return to their tribe and the marriage would be performed.

One condition remained. Running Deer would be required to give up his human form until the dog was captured. It would be immersed in the lake, and his ghost and the ghost of his beloved would together engage in the quest. On its successful conclusion they would both be restored to human form just as they had been when they parted before the great storm.

As the Great Spirit finished talking, a cloud like a heavy mist fell on the little island. Slowly, slowly, Running Deer saw the ghostly form of his beloved materialize out of the cloud. She was dressed all in white and her smile was radiant as she came toward him with arms outstretched. He ran to meet her, and even as they embraced, he looked over her shoulder and beheld the swamp spirits carrying his own body out into the lake, where they pushed it under the surface until he could no longer see any trace. Only several large bubbles marked the spot for a brief moment, and then even they were gone.

From that day to this, they say, on almost any night, but particularly when there is a full moon rising late, you can still see Running Deer and Moon Flower as they search for that celestial dog. Back and forth across what the white man calls Lake Drummond, they paddle their white canoe, searching, ever searching for the canine whose capture will return them to their lost happiness.

That is the ancient Indian legend, but many present-day people who live in or near the Great Dismal, as well as those sportsmen who are familiar with its ways, can and do vouch for the apparition.

Call it swamp gas, if you will. Call it a combination of late-rising mists and vivid imaginations or the terror which still inhabits such a place. The story still persists and is believed by many.

Thomas Moore, the famous Irish satirist and poet, visited the fledgling United States at some time between the American Revolution and the War of 1812. He very much wanted to see the swamp and the lake that were such a fascination for President Washington, Patrick Henry, and others, and he made a special effort to go there. He heard the legend of the white canoe and the Indian lovers, and it so impressed him that he lingered in the Great Dismal Swamp to gather more details. It is said that during this extension of his visit, he was caught in a terrible storm such as the one that had delayed Running Deer, and the Irishman was in great fear for his life. But people say that even as the very earth around him shook, great trees came crashing down, and the insane winds screamed and wailed, Thomas Moore sat down and wrote a beautiful poem about the Indian lovers.

Whatever the location and the exact circumstances of his setting quill to paper, it is certain that he did compose such a poem before he left America. This is his version of the legend:

A BALLAD — THE LAKE OF THE DISMAL SWAMP

by Thomas Moore

"They made her a grave too cold and damp
  For a soul so warm and true;

A *Dismal Swamp Love Story*

And she's gone to the Lake of the Dismal Swamp
Where all night long, by a firefly lamp,
   She paddles her white canoe.
And her firefly lamp I soon shall see,
And her paddle I soon shall hear;
   Long and loving our life shall be,
And I'll hide the maid in a cypress tree,
When the footstep of death is near."

Away to the Dismal Swamp he speeds,—
   His path was rugged and sore,

Through tangled juniper, beds of reeds,
Through many a fen where the serpent feeds,
   And man never trod before

And when on the earth he sank to sleep,
   If slumber his eyelids knew,
He lay where the deadly vine doth weep
Its venomous tear, and nightly steep
   The flesh with blistering dew!

And near him the she-wolf stirr'd the brake,
   And the copper-snake breathed in his ear,
Till he starting cried, from his dream awake,
"Oh when shall I see the dusky Lake,
   And the white canoe of my dear?"

He saw the Lake, and a meteor bright
   Quick over its surface play'd,—
"Welcome," he said, "my dear one's light!"
And the dim shore echo'd for many a night
   The name of the death-cold maid.

Till he hollow'd a boat of the birchen bark,

Which carried him off from shore;
Far, far he follow'd the meteor spark,
The wind was high and the clouds were dark,
    And the boat return'd no more.

But oft, from the Indian hunter's camp,
    This lover and maid so true
Are seen at the hour of midnight damp
To cross the Lake by a firefly lamp,
    And paddle their white canoe!

Do you suppose Moore saw something on the night when the terrible storm caught him in the Great Dismal Swamp?

The poet who composed such well-known works as "The Harp that Once through Tara's Hall" and the equally beautiful "The Last Rose of Summer" must surely have felt the presence of the young lovers.

He, for one, believed in them.

DANIEL KEATH

*N*AGS HEAD has been called "the best kept secret in North Carolina." For many years it was exactly that. Isolated, secluded, and wildly beautiful both in calm and in storm, it was known to relatively few people. From colonial times, down through World War I, and for years after that, there were only a few cottages on the ocean beach and a few more on the sound side. Except for those adventurous souls who would, from time to time, try to drive an automobile down the beach at low tide from Dam Neck far to the north, the only access was by one steamboat a day. It came down from Elizabeth City and returned thence before dawn on the following day.

All the "summer people" as well as most of the locals would meet the boat every afternoon to pick up mail and packages and newspapers and to see who got off the boat. The steamer *Trenton*, with Captain Martin Johnson at the wheel, was the weekday connection with the outside world for years, and on Sunday, the steamer *Vanscuiver* made the trip down and back on the same day. Other than an occasional excursion boat bringing a group of people to the beach for a single day, this was the way you got to and from Nags Head. Cottagers would not think of locking their doors, even at night, and you always knew, down to the last child and dog, exactly who was on the "island." If an emergency or tragedy occurred back home, the Coast Guard would come to your cottage in their pony cart and bring you the news.

These were the days after World War I and before the Great Depression that preceded World War II, and everything was bright and calm and serene. Even the infrequent "equinoctial storms," as hurricanes were called then, did not strike the terror that they do today. The buildings were erected in anticipation of such storms, and most of the cottages withstood them very well. The weatherwise fishermen and Coast Guardsmen could usually tell when such a storm was coming, and there was time and abundant help to prepare.

Houseguests would stay for a fortnight or a month, and most of the pleasures and entertainments were simple and wholesome. Saturday night movies were available over in Manteo, but you had to hire a boat to take you over there and bring you back.

The older teenagers and other unmarried folks tended to gather in groups, at least early in the evenings, and to enjoy group activities. The younger children, of course, would tag along after these groups until some of the married chaperones could convince them that it was time for them to retire to their respective cottages and turn in for the night.

One of these nocturnal group activities was the custom of the beach bonfire. When the wind was offshore, the men would dig a large hole in the sand of the flat beach, well away from the cottages, and build a large fire in it. Courting couples and other young people would gather around the fire as the stars came out and the moon rose out of the sea. There they would sing songs and roast weiners and toast marshmallows to their hearts' content. As the evening wore on and the fire died down to a soft glow, it was the inviolate custom for some member of the throng to tell a ghost story or a shipwreck story or a tale of some unexplained or mysterious happening.

One of the rules of the beach was that a newcomer or houseguest would be allowed exactly three such outings, and after that, he or she would be expected to tell the story of the evening. In the event of a refusal, the strong young men of the party would seize the rule-breaker and throw him or her, fully dressed, into the ocean. Not in deep water, mind you, but just in the shallow wash—to emerge thoroughly wet but otherwise unharmed.

One such houseguest was a young lawyer from the mountains of North Carolina named Charlie Yancey. He was very much enamoured of one of the prettiest young ladies in the summer colony and had frankly come a-courting, staying just a few cottages away and paying constant court to his lady love. The other swains were more than a little jealous of Yancey and just waited for the time when he would be called upon to provide the story at the bonfire. Surely no mountain man would be able to entertain the group, and they would be able to dampen his clothing, if not his ardor.

Well, the night finally came when Yancey had used up his three bonfires, and he was called upon to provide the story. The young man rose from his seat in the sand and moved around to the windward so that the smoke from the dying fire would not get in his eyes and he could see the faces of his audience more clearly.

"You all know," he began, "that I come from the mountains. I cannot match your stories of shipwrecks and pirates and such, but back in my hills we do have stories that are said to be true and that are strange and mystifying. I practice law in Rutherfordton, up in Rutherford County, and there is a tale that is well known up there and that many of the oldest residents swear is the whole truth and nothing but the truth.

"The courthouse and the jailhouse and the stocks were erected in Rutherfordton in 1784, and those same structures remained in use for many years. Right next to the south wall of the jailhouse was the gallows on which capital criminals were executed in those days. It had thirteen steps to the scaffold that supported the gibbet.

"Well, there was a fellow named Daniel Keath who lived in Cleveland County in the late 1800s. He was charged with murder in the death of a child named Alice Ellis. The evidence against Keath was pretty convincing, and the jury convicted him of murder in the first degree. Feeling ran so high that the trial had to be moved to Rutherford County. Keath maintained throughout the trial that he was innocent and that he was many miles away from the scene of the murder. He even presented witnesses who testified that they saw a man they thought was Keath in a neighboring town on the afternoon of the murder, but on cross-examination by the solicitor, they admitted that they could not be sure.

"Anyway, the jury believed the state's witnesses, and after a long and heated trial, they returned their guilty verdict and Keath was sentenced to be hanged. The case was appealed, but the appeals court could find no error in the trial, and the case was sent back down to Rutherford County in order that the sentence could be carried out.

"The execution date was set for December 11, 1880, and on that date at the appointed time, the condemned man was brought to the square to be hanged. He climbed the thirteen steps of the scaffold and refused the black hood and the blindfold that were offered him. Asked if he had anything to say before he was executed, Daniel Keath faced the crowd there assembled and in a strong, clear voice protested again that he was not guilty of the murder of the child. He told the people that they and the state were killing an innocent man and that his spirit would never rest until justice was done and his name cleared. When he had finished, the trap door was sprung, and in the words of the official records, 'Daniel Keath was hanged by the neck until he was dead.'

"The townspeople had witnessed hangings before, and they thought they were through with Daniel Keath, but they were wrong.

"Early the next morning, astounded early risers saw on the south wall of the jailhouse the shadow of the gallows and the gibbet just as plain as day. They also saw the shadow of Daniel Keath hanging from the rope and swaying gently in the breeze.

"The shadow of the dead man appeared on the next day and the next and the next, and on every day thereafter. The sheriff and his deputies and the hangman could do nothing to cause it to go away.

"Finally, they went to the extreme of tearing that jailhouse down. It was old and outmoded anyway, and they needed a new one. And besides, that action would surely get rid of the shadow of Daniel Keath. It did, all right, but people say that it did not get rid of the influence of the hanged man.

"The new jail was built some distance away, and in the place of the old jail they built some very attractive commercial property. But every single business that moved into the new structure for the next thirty years either failed or went bankrupt, or the owner died in a mysterious way.

"Long before that thirty years of blight ended, the courthouse itself (in which Keath had been tried and convicted and sentenced to die) burned on Christmas Day, 1907. There are those who say that this, too, was the act of Daniel Keath against those whom he claimed had unjustly taken his life."

As the young mountaineer finished his story and sat down again in the sand, there was complete silence on the part of his audience. Then, from the heart of the dying fire, there rose a sort of a cloud, as of rising steam from a wet or green fire log, and that cloud slowly took on the shape of a gallows. From that gallows dangled what appeared to be a rope, and from that rope there was suspended what looked to be the body of a man, swinging slowly back and forth. Then the whole thing quietly disappeared into the night sky.

No one applauded or even spoke for several minutes, but you can bet your boots that Charlie Yancey was not dipped in the ocean on that night.

To those who are skeptical of the story of the fate of Daniel Keath, take the time to look up the case in the court records. In the state capital of Raleigh you will find the library of the North Carolina Supreme Court.

In that library, in volume eighty-three, on page 626, you will find the reported case of *State v. Daniel Keath*.

Noted in the reasons why Keath requested a new trial, the court says: "2. Because the prisoner offered to prove by one J. Hicks, a witness for the defense, a conversation between the said Hicks and one Bridges of 28 January, 1880, at 'Burnt Chimney,' about eighteen miles from the place of the homicide, with regard to the person described in the testimony of Hicks given at the trial. The state objected, and the conversation was ruled out; to which the prisoner excepted."

After exhaustively examining all the evidence in the case, the supreme court concluded that there had been no error and that the jurors were justified in their verdict. The appellate court concludes: "The prisoner by their verdict had been justly doomed to the expiation of a crime characterized by the most brutal cruelty. The court finds NO ERROR."

Thus Daniel Keath's fate was sealed and the legend of the shadow was born.

A MODERN GHOST

*G*HOSTS, like nuggets of gold, are where you find them. There seems to be no particular habitat or locality where ghosts abound. It does seem to be the rule, though, that the older the town or community, the greater the likelihood of running across ghost stories.

There are literally hundreds of stories about ghosts of the long ago and ghosts in far-off places, but the accounts are usually frank hearsay and impossible to verify. It is a most unusual circumstance when one is able to document a tale of supernatural occurrences. It is even more rare to find hard-headed, practical businessmen who will look you square in the eye and tell you, not only that they have seen a ghost, but when and where and under what circumstances the sighting occurred.

Such is the case at hand.

When you think about it, it seems that "the original Washington," located on the broad waters of the Pamlico River in Beaufort County, North Carolina, might be a likely spot to evoke spirits. Older than our nation's capital city, Washington was a port of entry to this country as far back as colonial times. Sailing ships from the far corners of the world visited there regularly, and a busy trade was carried on with the West Indies and other islands in the Caribbean. It is established historical fact that the pirate Blackbeard visited Washington often, and that one of his several homes was located in Bath Town, just down the river a few miles from Washington. Today, a stroll along the restored waterfront and an examination of the handmade bricks comprising the walls of some of the old buildings will give you a sense of the town's antiquity.

In the more modern part of town is located a fine shopping center known as Washington Square Mall. The mall houses a number of large and completely stocked stores of various kinds operated by successful and hardworking owners and managers.

Typical of these establishments is a store owned and operated by one of the most respected businessmen in Washington. He is a highly literate person and also a strictly-business, no-nonsense type of merchant. If you had to pick one adjective that would best describe his standing, that adjective would most likely be "responsible."

Down the Pamlico River from Washington there is a series of exclusive riverfront residential developments, all bearing appropriate names and all fronting on the ever-widening Pamlico. Most of the mansions have large, green front yards sloping down to the water with little piers running out into the stream for the use of boaters, fishermen, and swimmers.

On May 27, 1980, shortly after ten o'clock P.M., our businessman was sitting on a bench on one of those piers in the development known as River Acres. He was relaxing and enjoying the beauty of a full moon rising over the river.

As he gazed idly at the other piers, his attention was

drawn by a burst of music and laughter just downstream from where he sat. There was another pier just to the east, and it was from there that the merriment seemed to come. Then, outlined against the rising moon, he saw the figure of a young woman dressed in a long, silver evening gown. She was quite alone, and he was close enough to see that she was barefoot.

The woman walked out along the pier at a leisurely pace as though she were taking an ordinary evening stroll. When she came to end of the structure, however, she did not stop or turn, but continued to walk out on thin air, still at the same leisurely pace, swinging her arms as she walked. To his amazement, our merchant was actually able to see the reflection of the moon on the water several feet under her figure. There was absolutely nothing there to support her weight. Further and further she went, until her figure disappeared out over the middle of the river. She did not fall or drop. She just faded away into the thin air and the river mist.

Fearing that a tragedy might have taken place, the businessman ran down the riverbank until he reached the house at the foot of the pier. All was dark there, but he beat on the door until lights came on in the house and the occupants came down and opened the door. Excitedly, he told them what he had just seen.

Smiling and patting him reassuringly on the shoulder, they said, "Don't worry about that. That's only Mrs. Mish and she will be back again next spring. She will never harm you, and she is free to come and go as she wishes." So saying, they went back into the house, and in a short time the lights inside again went out.

Still not convinced, our businessman walked out to the end of the pier and looked carefully around. There was nothing, absolutely nothing except a beautiful spring night and a calm, moonlit river flowing serenely toward the sea. Out in the middle of the Pamlico, a fish, bent on some unknown business of his own, jumped clear of the surface of the river and fell back with a splash.

Still not satisfied, the businessman looked into the matter the next day and found that most of the residents of the waterfront knew and were not afraid of Mrs. Mish. She had lived there years ago, they told him, and had been a well-liked and respected member of the community. One of her hobbies had to do with the history of the Indians who once inhabited that part of the state, and she had become convinced that a certain portion of the riverfront near where the pier was later built had been an Indian burial ground and was sacred to the tribe. She had stated her intention to conduct a dig on the spot and see what she could find, although she well knew the taboos the Indians were supposed to have placed on such prying.

On the eve of the dig she had given a party and had announced her plans. A full moon was shining then as it was on May 27, 1980,—the first full moon in May—and the night was beautiful. After a time, Mrs. Mish left the party and walked down toward the water's edge. When she did not return, the merrymakers went out to look for her, and they found her shoes placed neatly side by side at the water's edge as though she had gone wading. There were no tracks, either in or out of the water, and no sign of any struggle. Nothing except those two little shoes.

She was never seen again.

That is, she was never seen in human form again. But her spirit always returns on the first full moon in May and takes a solitary walk out the pier and into the mists of the Pamlico.

There is something strange and occult about that first full moon in May. Coastal people will tell you that there will be no softshell crabs in the spring until the first full moon in May, whether that be early or late in the month. After that moon, plenty of softshells. It is only in the softshell stage that the female crab is able to mate, and in some mysterious way, she seems to know just exactly when that moon occurs.

Did the ancient Indians attach special religious significance to that time of spring? Did their spirits resent the planned intrusion of modern men, especially in that holy time period? Did they take Mrs. Mish as a hostage because she knew too much about them and their burial ground?

Who knows?

So far as is known, Mrs. Mish never speaks on her annual visits to the Pamlico, nor is there a record of anyone trying to talk to her. What a tale she could tell if she would only talk!

Anyway, there it is. There you have a ghost with a name and a predictable time and place for annual appearances vouched for by some of the very best and most respectable people in the community.

What do you think?

SOME
CHOCOWINITY
GHOSTS

*T*HE LITTLE TOWN of Chocowinity in Beaufort County, North Carolina, boasts of at least two ghosts who frequent the vicinity. Chocowinity is named for an Indian tribe that called the area home many years before the War of American Independence. The town itself is much older than the era immediately following the Civil War, but the post-bellum period is the time frame in which the hauntings are said to have begun. The story of one of the ghosts involves some famous people who were participants in a major way in the history of the times. The other story concerns relative unknowns about whom very little is remembered other than their names.

The Reconstruction period following the War Between the States was a terribly sad and hard one for the people of the Tar Heel State, as it was for most of the South. The Confederate army had been defeated, and carpetbaggers, "bummers," and deserters from the Union army were a blight upon the economic, social, and political life of the region.

There were some bright spots, however. The surviving Confederates were coming home to take up their work on the farms and in the businesses, and the "flower of the South" were turning their attention to restoring normalcy.

One of these bright spots was the homecoming of

General J. Bryan Grimes. To quote the August 19, 1880, issue of the *Tarboro Southerner*, the general was "a brave officer, a hard fighter, a trusted leader of General Lee and emblazoned North Carolina's history with glory and heroism. He participated in all the important battles fought in Virginia and surrendered at Appomattox. It was there, when the negotiations for the surrender had been inaugurated, a charge and rebel yell was heard at the front. General Lee turned to an aide and asked, 'Who is that charging?' 'General Grimes' Division of North Carolinians,' was the reply. General Lee exclaimed: 'God bless the North Carolinians—they are the first and last in every charge!' "

Grimes was a returning hero to the people and proved himself to be no less a leader in the pursuit of peace than he was in battle. All the residents looked up to him and respected him, and he lived up to that respect. Even down to this day his descendants are among the most prominent lawyers and statesmen in the state. The little town of Grimesland was named for his family, and North Carolina has erected historical markers there commemorating his life and service.

On August 14, 1880, General Grimes had been attending a Democratic county convention in Washington, North Carolina, and was on his way home in his buggy, which was drawn by two spirited horses. With him was a young boy named Bryan Satterthwaite. The youngster was all of twelve years old at the time.

Before long the buggy was traveling the narrow road through Bear Swamp, some five miles from Washington. Suddenly, from somewhere within the dense undergrowth lining the sides of the rutted road, a shot rang out. General Grimes was struck by a single buck-shot, which, according to the *Tarboro Southerner*, "passed through the artery in the left arm and entered the body ranging in the direction of the right lung."

General Grimes died at the scene, and his body was taken to his plantation home to be prepared for burial.

Public indignation was extreme, and the hunt was on immediately for the assassin. Several people were sus-pect, but little could be proved although the investiga-tion was intense and lasted for weeks. Finally suspicion settled on one William Parker, a white man who had been in the area and had acted very suspiciously. He was indicted for murder, and the public feeling was running so high that the trial of the case was moved from Wash-ington to Williamston, North Carolina.

The trial was a celebrated one and lasted for weeks. Strong circumstantial evidence was presented against Parker, who decided not to take the witness stand on his own behalf. All the major newspapers of the South covered the trial. The reporter for the *Tarboro South-erner* seemed to sum up the situation when he reported to his paper during the time the jury was still out deciding the case: "Who was the assassin? There seems to be little diversity of opinion as to the prisoner's guilt, from an impartial and unprejudiced jury. But, Mr. Edi-tor, you are well aware that the two most uncertain things in life are the result of a town election and the verdict of a jury."

How right he was! The jury came back in and returned a verdict of Not Guilty. Parker was released to return to his home in the Chocowinity region. Although he often threatened to tell what he knew about the killing, he stoutly maintained that he was innocent.

Obviously, there was a considerable segment of public opinion that was not in agreement with Parker or with the jury. A short time later a party of several men (some of them from Parker's home community) called on him. They bound him securely in chains, took him to the drawbridge spanning the Pamlico River at nearby Washington, and there hanged him by the neck under the bridge until he was dead. The bridge tender, who went there the next morning to open the draw for a passing boat, found the body dangling with its feet almost in the water.

The older residents of Chocowinity insist that sometime later, a former slave confessed on his deathbed that it was he and not Parker who had shot the general, and that he had done so for revenge. It seems that General Grimes had been instrumental in obtaining a conviction of the brother of the ex-slave for burning his mill and that the brother had died in prison. They say that the ancient ex-slave's last words were, "There, Lord, I have confessed my sin. Now let me die in peace."

And so perhaps he did, but Parker was not so lucky. The people who live in the vicinity say that he still returns on moonlit nights. Of course, the old wooden drawbridge has long since been replaced by a steel and concrete structure, but the fishermen say that you can still see the body hanging underneath the bridge, you can still hear the clank of the chains that bound it, and you can even hear Parker repeat over and over again, "Not guilty; not guilty; not guilty."

The other Chocowinity ghost is said to be the spirit of

a carpetbagger who took up residence in the neighborhood just a short while after Parker was killed. He was quite a disturbing influence on the community and was heartily disliked by the local people.

Called simply "Joe Savage," he told no one where he came from nor whence his livelihood, but he was suspected of numerous thefts and illegal activities. He might have lived this down, however, had not a young woman accused him of rape. She told such a convincing story that the same group that had called on Parker also visited Savage and hanged him on the large holly tree under which the assault was said to have occured, and which still stands on the outskirts of Chocowinity.

Savage also protested his innocence to the end, but unlike Parker, he coupled his protests with a threat. If he were hanged, he said, his spirit would never rest until his innocence was proved, and terrible things would happen to each of the descendants of his killers to the third and fourth generation. The only way for those descendants to avoid the curse, he said, would be for each of them to come to that holly tree in the dark of the moon and there call upon Savage's spirit and apologize for the act of his ancestors.

Although it is said that one of the members of the hanging party lost his mind and died completely mad from worrying over these threats, it is not known exactly who the other members of the party were.

Some of the young people of the area claim to be worried lest the curse apply to them. To avoid it, they have gone to the tree in the dark of the moon and there apologized to the Savage spirit just in case some of their ancestors had been involved.

They vow that in each such case they have seen lights moving around in that holly tree and have heard moans and groans coming from the heart of the thick branches, but not one of them has ever been harmed. They keep returning and apologizing, year after year.

Their parents call it "just kid foolishness," but those kids continue to brave the darkness and the weird lights and sounds just to be on the safe side.

Why they keep going back is another question. Your guess is as good as mine.

MR. HAMILTON'S
LIGHT

*T*HE DIAMOND SHOALS lying off Cape Hatteras have long been infamous as "The Graveyard of the Atlantic." Literally hundreds of ships have been lost there, including the Union ironclad *Monitor*, which has only recently been discovered on the bottom of the sea in that area. Her anchor has been recovered by divers and is now at East Carolina University in Greenville, North Carolina, awaiting the recovery of other parts of the vessel.

Not only the *Monitor*, but also Spanish galleons, warships of many nations, countless pleasure craft, and many commercial vessels have met their end on the shoals. To this good day Cape Hatteras is dreaded by most mariners. One of the few reasons for coming close to it is the opportunity to catch the northward push of the Gulf Stream, which offers a great savings of time and fuel.

Almost as famous as the shoals is the Hatteras lighthouse, the tallest in the nation. This has recently received even more attention as the governor of North Carolina, the two senators from that state, and the millionaire owner of Grandfather Mountain, Mr. Hugh Morton, have joined with many other concerned people in an effort to save the historic light from encroachment by the stormy Atlantic.

Some of the older Outer Bankers still call the lighthouse "Mr. Hamilton's Light," and for very good reason. Alexander Hamilton, one of the founding fathers of our country, is said to be largely responsible for the construction of the very first Hatteras lighthouse.

Alexander Hamilton was born in 1755 in the Danish West Indies, the illegitimate son of Rachel Fawcett Lavien, who had left her husband to become the common-law wife of one James Hamilton. By this Scottish merchant she bore Alexander and an older brother, James. In 1765, the boys' father up and left Rachel and her two illegitimate children to fend for themselves as best they could. Rachel died in February of 1768. After her death, Alexander became a clerk in the business of a New York merchant named Nicholas Cruger, who operated a trading firm in St. Croix. Young Hamilton prospered in this apprenticeship and was soon running the business.

When a terrible hurricane all but destroyed St. Croix, Alexander, who had always had a way with words, wrote such a brilliant description of the storm that his pastor arranged to have it published in the *Royal Danish American Gazette*. Other merchants in the Indies were so impressed with his brilliance that they made up a fund to send him to New York to study law. He had always said that he wanted to make politics his life work.

In the late fall of 1772, just three years before the battles of Lexington and Concord, the young man took ship for New York. Off Cape Hatteras his ship ran into a terrible storm, and young Alexander became so seasick he thought he would surely die. To make matters worse, the ship caught fire and had to be hove to and anchored in that treacherous sea until the fire could be controlled. For twenty-four hours Hamilton aided the crew by being a member of a bucket brigade, which brought sea water from overside in buckets and passed it, hand to hand, until it could be thrown on the blazing cargo. To add to the terror, the ship's captain did not know where they were nor how close the deadly shoals were to the leeward.

When the fire was finally contained and the storm had subsided enough so that the vessel could once again get under way, our young traveler swore an oath. On the memory of his dead mother he swore that if he should ever achieve a position of influence in the new land, he would see to it that a lighthouse marked that dangerous spot. Thus all future mariners could be warned to give it a wide berth.

Of course, Hamilton went on to become one of the giants of American history. He was caught up in the American Revolution and other famous historical events. He served in the Continental Congress and later became a member of the United States Congress. True to his word, he ramrodded through Congress the bill that, in 1794, authorized the construction of the first Hatteras lighthouse. It was a structure some 120 feet in height and was the marvel of its day. Lighted with kerosene, it served its purpose well until the sea claimed it, and it had to be blown up after a new lighthouse was built. The old foundations are still there, however, for visitors to see, and the old-timers still call the Hatteras light "Mr. Hamilton's light" in memory of that famous man who did not forget to keep his vow.

Perhaps Mr. Hamilton continues to watch over his light, for it has continued to burn—from one structure or another—despite the threats of time and tides.

The present lighthouse was built in 1870 and is some 208 feet in total height. In 1935 this lighthouse became endangered by the encroaching sea, and a steel tower was built back in the woods to replace it. The Civilian Conservation Corps came on the scene about then under the aegis of President Franklin Delano Roosevelt. One assignment for those work crews was to try to halt the inroads of the Atlantic and preserve the lighthouse. Saved from unemployment and the bread lines, the eager young men worked hard to accomplish what engineers said couldn't be done.

Out in front of the threatened lighthouse, the crews built sand fences of scrap timber and yaupon and merkle bushes from the marshes behind Hatteras. These effectively trapped the blowing sand and built up little mounds where the fences were covered. The crews then built more fences to seaward—more fences and still more, and the sea was beaten back to the point where it no longer threatened the tower. There was plenty of scrap timber from former hurricanes, plenty of wind to drift the sand, and plenty of merkle and yaupon with which to form the fences. It was one work-relief program that worked.

Even so, the powers that be still would not consent to reactivating the lighthouse but insisted on keeping the light on the iron skeleton tower back in the woods. That was when Ben Dixon MacNeill came on the scene. A brilliant writer who spent his adult life on the Outer Banks among the people he loved, he mounted an almost one-man campaign to reactivate the light. So fluent was he and so persuasive that he finally saw his dream come true, and the light still shines from the lighthouse.

Once again the sea has come threatening, but this time, it appears that a new invention called Seascape will be able literally to turn the tide. This artificial seaweed is being planted in increasing quantities just offshore from the light and is apparently building up the beach so that mother sea is once again retreating.

One strange footnote needs to be added to this brief history of Mr. Hamilton's light.

Alexander Hamilton, who worked so hard to bring the light to Hatteras, was killed in 1804 in a duel with Aaron Burr. Ironically, Aaron Burr's only child, his beloved Theodosia, is believed to have perished in North Carolina's coastal waters, almost within sight of Mr. Hamilton's light.

But that is another story.

THE
HOLY GHOST
SHELL

*F*OR LITERALLY hundreds of years, beachcombing and shell collecting have been pleasant hobbies for both visitors and permanent residents of North Carolina's Outer Banks. Children and adults alike enjoy searching for the beautiful shells found in abundance on the seashore. Some people have amassed large collections. There are even shops that specialize in nothing but shells, both local and foreign.

One of the most popular of these shells is known as the sand dollar. Circular in shape and of various sizes, this skeleton of a small marine animal bleaches out to a pleasing whiteness on the beach and makes an interesting decoration or conversation piece. In the old days they were quite easy to find, but with the advent of millions of tourists and surf fishermen, they are becoming harder and harder to come by. It is now a fairly rare occurrence to find a perfect and unbroken sand dollar on the beach.

Most beach visitors know the sand dollar, but many of them have never heard the legend of that particular seashell, a legend which dates back to the early beginnings of English efforts to colonize this "goodliest soile under the cope of heaven."

When Amadas and Barlowe were sent to explore the land in April of 1584, they brought with them a sizable force of Englishmen to conduct the exploration. It is said that one of the sailors was a man named Henry Fowlkes who was, by nature, of a religious bent. He had even studied to be a priest in the newly formed Anglican Church.

Fowlkes was much impressed with the beauty of the land he was visiting, and he loved to take long, solitary walks along the golden beaches to meditate and to commune with his God. The local Indians were quite friendly and he had no fear of them, but he did not know that the Outer Banks, even then, were visited by upland tribes for the wonderful hunting and fishing they knew they would find. Some of these visitors came from the Iroquoian tribes far to the west, and they were much more warlike and fierce than the local Algonquins. As luck would have it, Fowlkes happened one day on one of these hunting parties and was promptly taken prisoner.

When the hunting party returned to their own village, they took the Englishman with them, and there he remained as a slave, as spring and summer faded into fall and winter. In time he learned the Iroquoian language and taught some of them to speak English, but he was looked down upon as a "squaw man," who was relegated to the most menial tasks and who could expect nothing but contempt.

After he had taught them his language, the Englishman began to teach the tribe about Jesus and about his coming to save all mankind, including the Indians. He told them of the crucifixion and the resurrection of the Savior. As his lessons progressed, his audience became larger and larger. Some of the women began to inquire how they too could secure this salvation and life eternal. Even the fierce braves began to be interested and to ask searching questions.

The medicine men were infuriated. They saw a threat in this Englishman and his new religion. They greatly feared that their influence would fade away if the Indians accepted Christianity. These ritualists were men of considerable power in the tribe. Using the threat of vengeance by the forest spirits if these teachings were allowed to continue, they persuaded the chiefs to sentence Fowlkes to death for heresy. They insisted that he be taken back to the spot where he had been captured and there be beaten to death with their ceremonial clubs.

Accordingly, in the month of April in the year 1585, a party of braves carried the slave back to the very spot on the beach where he had been found. He was made to kneel in the wet sand, and the medicine men gathered around with their clubs, waiting for the Indian king to strike the first blow.

"Now, white man," intoned the king, "your God and your Jesus-brave know where to find you. Your Holy Ghost must know that this is the spot from which we took you. Call on your gods, and if they are as powerful as you say, ask them for a sign. Give us a sign from nature as our Great Spirit does for us when we pray. Do this and we will release you. Pray, bearded-face! Pray for a sign or you die!"

Believing that death was imminent, Fowlkes clasped his hands and prayed with all his might that he be delivered from dying on this foreign shore, never to see his beloved England again. He was man enough and

Christian enough to conclude his prayer with the very words of our Savior, "Father, if it be thy will, let this cup pass from me. Nevertheless, not my will but thine be done."

Snarling, a medicine man kicked the kneeling slave in the face and sent him sprawling into the sand. "He speaks of a cup," sneered the Indian. "Let him drink from the cup of death."

As he struggled to rise from the sand, Fowlkes' hand closed around a large sand dollar. He had not seen such a seashell before, as they are common only on the sandy beaches of North America. He gazed upon it with awe.

"See, see," he shouted, holding the shell up before the chief's face. "Here is your sign. See how this strange shell shows forth the very things I told you about my Lord. See the circular shape like the crown of thorns. See the five slashes—they represent the thorns that pierced His brow. See the five marks in the center of the shell, which show the five wounds my Savior received on the cross. Here is your sign. Only see. See and believe!"

Taking the shell in his trembling hands, the chief turned it over and over and examined if from every angle. As a frequenter of this coast he had seen many of these shells and had wondered about the markings but had never had anyone try to explain them to him. Here, indeed, was the "sign from nature" he had demanded of the white man.

The head shaman was staring open-mouthed in amazement, not knowing what to say. The chief turned to hand him the shell, and in the exchange between the hands of the two, the fragile shell broke in half. Out fell several little things that looked exactly like little white doves.

"There is the sign of the Holy Ghost," exulted the prisoner. "This is not the Holy Ghost itself but is a sign—a sign using the image of that same white dove that descended bringing the Comforter to the people until my Lord's coming again."

The legend concludes that the tribesmen then turned and fled the beach and returned with all haste to their village, leaving the Englishman alone upon the strand. It is also said that this may be one explanation of the smattering of Christianity that the early settlers found extant among the inland Indians.

Fowlkes lost no time in walking down the beach to a point opposite Roanoke Island, where he found, to his joy, that Sir Richard Grenville had just arrived with some 600 men and would soon return to England. Sir Richard welcomed Henry Fowlkes as an additional hand on board one of his ships and carried him back to his native land, where Fowlkes entered the Anglican priesthood and spent the rest of his life serving churches in Devon and Yorkshire. He is said to have carried many sand dollars with him and to have used them in his sermons.

Now, you may know that the sand dollars found on the Atlantic and Pacific shores of this country are really specimens of the various thin, circular echinoderms of the order *Clypeastrina*, especially *Echinarachnius parma*, of sandy ocean bottoms of the northern Atlantic and Pacific. But ask any knowledgeable coastal child what one is, and like a little cherub, he will explain to you that it is really the Holy Ghost shell and that his grandfather has shown him the marks of the thorns and the wounds. If it is a whole shell, he might break it in two for you and let you see the little snow-white doves that come from the inside.

Imagery? Superstition? Well, now, don't be too sure. "There are more things in this world than are dreamed of in your philosophy."

THE GREAT SERPENT
OF THE
FRESH PONDS

*B*ACK IN the early 1900s, a pleasant Outer Banks pastime was to take long walks, either on the beach or up through Nags Head Woods. A popular destination for a stroll was the area of the Fresh Ponds, very near Kill Devil Hill.

This group of ponds is an extremely interesting phenomenon in a region of many natural wonders. Located just a short distance from the salty Atlantic Ocean, with neither a visible source nor outlet, these ponds contain only fresh water, usually very cold. The largest pond is quite deep and once contained brown trout and other fish normally found only in the mountains. Geologists theorize that the ponds are fed by aquifers, or underground rivers, beginning in the mountains and running all the way to the coast. When the water surfaces at this particular spot, the sandy terrain absorbs the natural overflow, creating the smaller ponds and settling banks. The mountain fish that once lived in the pond are thought to have been swept down from the mountains in the underground rivers. What other unexpected creatures dwell in these fresh waters, and what mysterious source brought them there, is the subject of at least one tale the Outer Bankers tell.

The story concerns two young boys, whom we shall call Jethro and Silas. The boys were staying with their families for the summer at the old Tony House hotel on the "sound side" at Nags Head. Although some five years separated them in age, they were close friends and co-adventurers in many an undertaking in and around that bucolic place.

One outing the boys had planned that summer was a fishing excursion to the Fresh Ponds. When the appointed date arrived, Jethro and Silas set out in the early morning, equipped not only with fishing poles and lines but with a large shotgun as well. Jethro thought that the gun might be needed in the long walk through the untamed woods. However, that walk was made without incident.

To reach the large pond, they had to traverse a reedy glade containing several live oaks so huge and so old that they almost certainly had been there when only the Indians had roamed those banks and the white man had never been heard of.

About halfway across the glade, Silas, the younger boy, screamed in terror and pointed with a trembling hand at one of the giant trees. There, protruding from a large hole in the tree trunk about five feet above the ground, was the head of the largest snake either one of them had ever seen. Its forked tongue flicked in and out of its cruel mouth.

Silas would have fled at top speed from such a menacing sight, but Jethro was made of sterner stuff, and he took hold of his young companion and wrestled him to the ground. When he had soothed his partner's fears somewhat, the older boy arose, loaded his shotgun with buckshot, and calmly proceeded to blow the head off the snake.

The lads then circled the tree, and there, at ground

93

level and protruding from another hole in the trunk of the tree, was the writhing tail of the snake.

Screwing their courage to the sticking point, our travelers laid hold of the tail and dragged the long body of the dead serpent out into the open. Its tail still twitched back and forth.

Forgetting about any fishing after that, the boys dragged their quarry over to the lifesaving station on the beach. The station keeper hitched up the pony cart, and the two boys and their snake were transported back to the Tony House.

The dead snake caused a sensation. The headless body measured over six feet in length. Many of the local residents stated that they had heard of such a snake and that it was rumored to have killed and eaten many small animals, including some young goats and several dogs.

When the carcass was stretched out on a long bench, onlookers could see a large swelling in its midsection. The hotel cook proceeded to cut open the snake and to take from its stomach an object that looked like a huge egg. It was oval in shape and about half the size of a football. It seemed to glow with an eerie and sinister light all its own.

No one present knew what sort of egg this could be, so they sent for a local character known only as Old Henry, who was supposed to have traveled many times around the world and who possessed a vast store of knowledge. He eked out a bare living doing handyman jobs around the hotel and the summer cottages and was said to be able to answer almost any question if plied beforehand with two cocktails to refresh his memory.

Duly ensconced in the Tony House bar and supplied

with two large cocktails, he inquired what the surrounding crowd wanted of him. He was shown the egg-shaped object and told of the circumstances surrounding its discovery.

"Why, that's an auk's egg," he cried in astonishment. "There's only one other of these in the whole world and that's in the British Museum. It is said to bring the owner nothing but disaster unless it is returned to the place where it was found. Take it back! Take it back!" With that, Old Henry climbed down hastily from the barstool and ran out the door of the hotel and off in the direction of the woods.

It was agreed that Jethro and Silas should make the decision as to what to do with the egg. The boys took the advice of Old Henry and made plans to return the egg to the Fresh Ponds immediately.

Early the next morning they made their way back to the place where they had first encountered the snake. Taking a small boat they found tied to the shore, they paddled out to the middle of the pond. There they proceeded to roll the egg over the side and into the water.

As they watched, the egg began to glow ever brighter with an illumination that seemed to come from within. Slowly, slowly, it sank into the depths of that pond, growing dimmer and dimmer as it sank, until finally it vanished altogether.

The skin of the huge snake was nailed to the side of one of the outbuildings at the Tony House. Parents often hinted to young Bankers that the snake was not really dead and that it had an appetite for naughty children. Although the skin finally disappeared one night during a particularly violent storm, the tale of the

Fresh Ponds Serpent still remains in the memory of the native folk, and it is still used on occasion to scare coastal children into obedience.

For some older residents, however, there is more to the story than a caution for disobedient children. According to them, the great egg is still in the large pond and has developed into a reliable prophet of disaster.

Upon irregular occasions, they say, but always at the stroke of midnight, a strange glow will emanate from the largest pond and grow brighter by the minute until the egg surfaces and breaks cleanly in two, each half riding the water like a boat.

From one of those halves, the mature great auk itself will materialize and take flight back and forth with mournful cries over the pond. Ten or twelve times it will cross the water before settling into the other half of the egg. The two halves then slowly reunite, encasing the huge bird. Believers in this tale insist that when the union of the two halves is complete and the great fowl is safely inside once again, the egg will gradually sink back into the depths, the glow growing dimmer and dimmer until it vanishes altogether.

Scoffers answer that the great nocturnal bird is nothing more than a large brown pelican seeking new fishing grounds and that the eerie subaquatic light is only an errant moonbeam aided by vivid imaginations.

"If that be so," the traditionalists reply, "why is it that exactly twenty-one days after every manifestation, some terrible storm or hurricane will scourge the area, leaving death and destruction in its wake?"

What do you think? Pelican or prophet?

THE MATTAMUSKEET APPLE

*I*N HYDE COUNTY in eastern North Carolina, there is a place called Lake Mattamuskeet. Long known to the Indians as a wonderful hunting and fishing place, it is thought to have been created by a fire, which burned out the rich peat and formed the basin for the lake. There is an Indian legend about the fire and the lake, but that is another story.

This folktale concerns another phenomenon found in the same location. On the shores of Lake Mattamuskeet there is to be found an apple called the Mattamuskeet apple. It apparently cannot be grown with any success anywhere else, but it is abundant around that lake. It is a rather small apple and it matures late, but it is of exceptional sweetness. It is highly prized by hunters and nature watchers who visit that area, and the wildlife feeds on it with gusto. The tree itself is rather small but is usually laden with fruit.

The name "Mattamuskeet," is a descriptive Indian term composed of two Algonquian words, "matta," meaning near, and "muskeet," meaning a lowland densely covered with brush and thickets. The word "muskeg" used by Indians in the northern part of our country apparently comes from the same origin, as it means practically the same thing. Thus the word means, quite literally, "Near the place of low-lying land covered with thick underbrush and thickets."

Long before the white man first came to America, there lived near this lush hunting ground a tribe of Algonquian Indians called the Machapunga. They had the usual tribal structure of the king, or weroance, and the medicine men—priestly sorcerers who ruled over the secular and the medico-religious lives of the other tribesmen. The medicine men were drawn from the young braves who volunteered for rigorous training as such. Only the brightest and most courageous were selected for such training.

One such brave was Swimming Bear, a youth who longed with all his heart to become a medicine man and who studied diligently to learn the many things such a priest was expected to know. He learned, for instance, that a hunter was required by the Great Spirit to apologize to a deer he had just killed. Immediately upon the death of the deer, a woods-spirit called Little Deer would appear on the scene and inquire of the slain deer's spirit if such an apology had been made by the hunter. If so, Little Deer would retire to the woods. If not, he would follow the trail of the hunter back to his village and, as punishment, would inflict rheumatism upon him. This could only be cured by long and involved incantations by the medicine man. Ulcers, he learned, were treated with a pack of doaty corn and some down from a turkey's rump.

These and many other remedies and ceremonies Swimming Bear learned, and the medicine men who taught him declared that he was one of the brightest students they had ever had. The ordeal of the sweating-house he endured with stoicism, and his ceremonial dances were marked with vigor and imagination, but one thing he lacked. No one could become a full-fledged medicine man unless and until he had had two visitations from the Great Spirit and had thereby accomplished two miracles. Swimming Bear prayed frequently for these visitations.

One night, so the story goes, the student was fast asleep when suddenly there appeared before him the Great Spirit to whom he had prayed. At that time, the old chief of Swimming Bear's tribe was ill and was constantly getting worse instead of better in spite of the efforts of the medicine men. No one seemed able to cure him. The vision told Swimming Bear that he should go to the place of the Ascapernong on the shores of the great sea water and there seek the cure for his chief. "ascapo" meaning "baytree" and "nong" meaning "the place of" in their language, the lad knew exactly where he was directed to go.

Launching his canoe, he went across the broad sound to what is now the Outer Banks of North Carolina. Beaching his craft on the sound shore, he walked across to the ocean where he found the waves actually breaking upon the luxuriant vines of the grape we still call the Scuppernong. He ate his fill of the delicious grapes and lay down in the shade of a tree, where he promptly fell asleep. Sure enough, the Great Spirit reappeared in a dream and directed him to harvest the leaves of the tree under which he slept and from them to brew a tea. This tea would be the long-sought cure for the king. The legend tells us that Swimming Bear obeyed, and the king was cured.

From that day forward, the leaves of that tree were used by the Indians and by the white settlers who followed them to make the tea that they say has almost magical curative powers. We know the tree as the yaupon or yeopon. Some of the early Outer Bankers made a living out of baling the branches and leaves of the yaupon tree and shipping them to Norfolk and Philadelphia, where they were in great demand. Yaupon tea is available today on our Outer Banks if you know where to look.

As may be imagined, Swimming Bear was quite a hero after this exploit, but he still lacked that second visitation from the Great Spirit before he could become a full-fledged medicine man. That visit was not long in coming.

Once again as Swimming Bear slept and dreamed, the Great Spirit appeared to him. This time he was directed to set out in his boat upon the waters of Lake Mattamuskeet and to take with him his bow and just one arrow, as well as a lighted torch from the council fire of the tribe. The arrow was not to be a hunting arrow but a fire arrow such as the Indians used to set fire to the houses of their enemies when attacking their towns. Once on the lake, he was to ignite his arrow and fire it at the first moving bird he saw. If his aim was true, he was to take the quarry to the council lodge and there open its craw, burying the contents in the ground beside the lodge.

Swimming Bear did exactly as he was told. The first fowl he saw at the lake was a wild goose flying extremely low and skimming the water in his direction. The aspirant to the priesthood lighted the tip of his fire arrow, and taking careful aim although his hands were trembling, he fired his arrow straight and true into the flying target.

Upon opening the craw of the goose, he found therein a peculiar seed, the likes of which he had never seen before. He took the seed and painstakingly planted it near the council lodge. He watered the spot and kept it shaded and tended it carefully until the seed sprouted and grew into a small tree, which bore the very first Mattamuskeet apple. The offspring from that first tree spread and multiplied until the little trees ringed the entire lake, where they remain until this good day to be eaten and enjoyed by humans and wildlife alike. These Indians had never seen an apple before, nor any fruit like it, although they enjoyed numerous melons. Needless to say, the little apple was revered for many years as a gift directly from the Great Spirit and it was never wasted. Today it is relished as an exceptionally good apple and is served in many ways by the local housewives.

If you are nature lover enough to visit this wonderful wild game preserve and see its numerous eagles and bears and bobcats and deer, and if you are smart enough to time your visit for the late summer or early fall, try to obtain some of these apples. You will find them a taste treat. If you take the seeds back home, though, and try to start your own orchard, the odds are strongly against your having much success. The Mattamuskeet apple seems to remain an exclusive blessing for the land on which it was bestowed—the land near the Muskeet.

THE FIRE BIRD

*M*ANY MOONS before Christopher Columbus set sail on his first voyage of discovery across the Atlantic Ocean, eastern North Carolina was populated by several tribes of native Indians. The various tribes of the Algonquian nation lived on the northeastern coastal section, while to the south and west the tribes of the Iroquoian and Siouan nations were in control.

Even if they occasionally engaged in warfare, relations between the nations were generally peaceful, and although they spoke different languages, they shared many traditions and beliefs. They all believed in the Great Spirit and in the Indian versions of heaven and hell. In addition, the woods and streams were believed to be inhabited by both good and evil spirits. An Indian's success or failure, sickness or health depended in great part on which spirit was able to attain mastery over him, although the one Great Spirit ruled over all.

One of the tribes of coastal Indians was known as the Roanocs. This tribe's principal town stood just about where the village of Wanchese now stands on the southern tip of Roanoke Island. Westward from their home island lay an extremely large and desolate swamp which was (and still is) an extremely fearsome place. It was a wilderness of swamp and marsh with extensive areas of quicksand where a man could sink from sight in minutes, never to be seen again. Although they sometimes hunted on its edges, the Roanocs avoided that area, preferring to detour around it on long journeys in their canoes. Even to this day, there are vast areas that, so far as is known, have never felt the foot of a human being. It is still very much the deep woods.

In this land of quaking earth there were huge snakes and other fearsome and dangerous creatures. The land was taboo, and no brave in his right mind would even think of hunting there. Further, it was believed to be the home of the great fire bird. This awful creature had the form of a huge vulture with eyes and nostrils that spouted flame and large, cruel talons with which it caught its prey. Where its shadow fell on the earth, the crops would fail and the people would become sick with a terrible illness. Its glance was said sometimes to cause instant death. Its presence drove away all the game and fish upon which the tribes depended. Jet black with the exception of the fire in its eyes and the flame spouting from its mouth, it cruised night and day over the land, hunting for small children, whom it would seize and devour. The entire Algonquian nation was terrorized by this malevolence to the point where they were often afraid to go outdoors to hunt or fish or tend their crops.

Fearing the complete destruction of all their people, the various chiefs of the Algonquins called for a great tribal council to be held in the home village of the Currituck tribe to devise a way to destroy this evil menace. Each tribe sent its bravest and strongest man to that council, and the old chief of the Roanoc tribe chose young Silver Arrow to represent him. Silver Arrow was not only the greatest hunter and fisherman of the tribe; he was also recognized as the wisest in council and the most fearless in battle, a worthy representative of the Roanocs.

The council met with great pomp and ceremony, and all of the tribes of the area were represented. Many plans were advanced for destroying the fire bird, but none of them seemed practical, and one after another they were discarded. The council dragged on for days and weeks as the delegates became more and more discouraged.

While he was there, Silver Arrow met the beautiful daughter of the Currituck chief, a girl named Morning Star, and the two proceeded to fall in love. Silver Arrow went to the old chief and asked for his daughter's hand in marriage, but the old man shook his head sadly and told Silver Arrow why such a union could never be.

Some time before, the chief had been captured when his hunting party had strayed into the land of the Iroquois. Their medicine man would have had him put to death had not the Iroquoian chief, a man called Evil Eyes, intervened and saved his life. This chief was known for his cruelty and sadistic nature and had earned his name from his apparent ability to paralyze with the force of his evil stare. His unusual act of mercy toward the Currituck chief was really an act of barter; he requested, and was promised, the hand of the beautiful Morning Star in marriage. The Currituck chief would not break his promise, and Evil Eyes was coming to Currituck in two moons to claim his bride. Only death (the chief's own, his daughter's, or Evil Eyes') could release him from his promise. The Iroquois were strong, and repudiation of the betrothal would result in a bloody war.

Silver Arrow and Morning Star were desolate. They went to the forest clearing by the broad water, where the Currituks were accustomed to go to communicate with the spirits, and there implored the Great Spirit's help. After many such pleas, the spirit told them that they should go back to the land of the quaking earth where the evil fire bird had its home. There they should invoke the good spirit of the swamp and ask for help. They were told that Chief Evil Eyes was in league with the fire bird and that the swamp spirit might be willing to help with both problems.

With great fear and misgiving, the young lovers did as they were told. Not knowing whether they would ever come back alive, they went into the great swamp of the quaking earth and found a huge cypress tree growing on a tiny hummock or island. Kneeling before this likely shrine, they prayed to the good swamp spirit for help.

As they were praying, a mysterious green light began to suffuse the whole landscape. It grew brighter and brighter and seemed to focus on the cypress tree before which they knelt. As the brilliance increased, there appeared in the very center of the glow the form of the good spirit of the swamp. The spirit asked the reason for the presence of the young lovers in that awful swamp, and they poured out their hopes and their fears and begged for help in solving their two problems.

The swamp spirit listened carefully and asked a few questions about how they had come to find out that Chief Evil Eyes was really an ally of the evil fire bird.

Finally the spirit agreed to help. It would provide aid and a way to cure both evils, but there was a great price. Silver Arrow and Morning Star had to promise that they would give their firstborn to the spirit, who would change the child into a great white bear. This bear would roam the forests and swamps to protect the Indians from other monsters that might come along in the future. It would help drive away the evil spirits that caused such monsters and protected them. To this costly bargain the lovers agreed, and the green light began to fade away as the form of the good spirit slowly ascended toward the top of the great cypress.

They had hardly gotten to their feet from their kneeling when there came a great, ear-splitting scream. With a great whistling sound, the evil fire bird swooped down upon them, fire spurting from its mouth and nostrils. It seized Silver Arrow by the nape of his neck in its great, cruel claws and soared away with him toward the very center of the forbidden swamp.

Morning Star did not know what to do. She somehow felt that she should not desert her lover, so she ran after the fire bird. The water and marsh got deeper and deeper as she ran, until she was almost waist deep in the mire. Then, as though lifted by some giant hand, she soared into the air above the tops of the trees and was carried farther and farther into the swamp.

In the distance she saw the pall of smoke from the underground fire of which her elders had told her, a fire that had been burning for many years. Suddenly and without warning, Morning Star was deposited in a clearing quite near the flames of the peat fire, and the heat and the odor were so intense that she could scarcely get her breath.

Then she saw the nest of the fire bird. It was as horrible to behold as the fire bird itself, and Morning Star was made sick at her stomach by the sight. Located high in a tree, it was made of the muscles of Indian braves of many tribes and was lined with the skeletons and skulls of Indian children it had eaten. Inside the nest there were three baby fire birds, each as hideous and sickening as the bird that had carried Silver Arrow away. Not yet able to fly, they screamed and hissed and opened their ugly mouths toward the sky.

Just at that moment, the great fire bird appeared with the girl's lover still in its claws. Seeing the awful nest, the young brave struggled and twisted with all his strength and finally broke free from the claws of the monster. He fell free, but he landed squarely in the nest of the awful bird. With a mocking laugh, the fire bird wheeled and flew away, leaving the Indian as food for the three young monsters. The three baby birds attacked Silver Arrow all at once, slashing him with their beaks and claws.

Morning Star could do nothing as she watched her brave fighting for his life. She knew in her heart that he would either be killed and eaten by the beasts or that the young birds would somehow be destroyed and the fire bird would then have to leave to find a safer place to build its nest. All day long the battle continued, but as evening grew near, Silver Arrow was finally able to overcome all three of the evil creatures and kill them in the nest. He tore their hearts out and ripped off their skins, and then, to make doubly sure they were gone, he dropped their remains over the side of the nest and into the raging peat fire burning below. The exhausted brave sank down to the floor of the nest. Below him, Morning Star made her bed out of the soft mosses and rushes she found growing on the forest floor.

With morning, the good spirit of the swamp returned and told the young couple that their troubles were almost over. The fire bird had seen what had happened and realized that her days of terrifying the Algonquins had come to an end. Now that her nest had been discovered and her young killed, she must find a new territory far, far away, for she could never return to that part of the land. As the huge bird flew away she swooped down and picked up old Chief Evil Eyes and carried him off with her forever. Somehow, she seemed to blame him for her misfortunes, and she seemed determined that he should share them.

The spirit told the young couple that they must now go with haste back to the spot where they had first sought help. A home had been prepared for them there, but they must hurry because a great hurricane was on its way. They did as they were told and found to their delight that the same spirit had prepared a genuine love nest for them high in the cypress tree. The cozy nest was roofed with the reeds and willows that grew in the marsh so that the lovers would be protected from the coming storm.

Then the hurricane struck. The wind howled and the rain fell without stopping for many days on end. The large cypress bent and swayed before the fury of the storm, but the couple's refuge remained intact, and they remained safe and warm and dry. They spent many days making love in their hideaway, and the storm-filled hours seemed to fly by.

Finally the hurricane was over, and the young couple descended from their hiding place. They made their way together back to the home villages of both their tribes and told what had happened. With the blessings of both chiefs, they were married and settled down in their own little dwelling in the hometown of the Roanocs.

In due time their home was blessed with their first little papoose, a fine healthy boy. They kept their bargain with the good spirit of the swamp and gave the youngster over to the spirit, who immediately changed him into a large, snow-white bear.

As the spirit had promised, the bear roamed the swamps and marshes of that part of the land, keeping watch against evil spirits and protecting any Indians who somehow managed to stray into the deep woods. That didn't happen often. Old taboos never die, and there were many other hunting grounds where the game was plentiful now that the evil fire bird had gone away. The white bear was sighted from time to time, but he was left strictly alone to continue his good work—which they say he does to this day.

Biologists tell us that albinism can occur in any animal, although it is more rare in some than in others. It is entirely within the realm of possibility that the white animal you saw loping through the woods as you drove your car near Engelhard or East Lake along the edge of the great marsh was an albino bear. Or it may have been the first born of Silver Arrow and Morning Star, looking for some Indians to protect.

In either case, if I were you, I would leave it strictly alone and not try to pursue it into the marsh. Remember, there are many places in that marsh where the foot of man has never trod. There have been unexplained disappearances and other mysterious happenings in that fey place of unknown and unfamiliar dangers.

It would be best to emulate the Algonquins and leave it strictly alone.

THE SEA HAG

*T*O *THE SOUTH* of Hatteras Island and across Hatteras Inlet lies the beautiful and, at one time, barely accessible island and village of Ocracoke. Even farther south and across Ocracoke Inlet lies the wildly beautiful and still isolated Portsmouth Island, as well as what remains of the ancient town of Portsmouth.

Even though some of the buildings remain in a state of good preservation and some are being restored, there is little there now to show the visitor of the once-bustling port that was one of the most important ports of entry in the state. In colonial times there were many houses there, and residents and visitors could take advantage of an infirmary, a number of stores, barracks for troops, ship chandler's shops, and several saloons. Extensive docks lined the sound shorefront, and most of the freight that came into northeastern North Carolina by sea came through the port of Portsmouth.

It was long before even this early time, however, that the events related in this story are said to have come to pass. In those times most of the island was covered with a dense forest of cedar and live oak and a thick under-brush of merkle bushes. Yaupon grew there in abundance, and some of the inhabitants of Portsmouth Village supplemented their living from the sea with the sale of bales of yaupon, which was much in demand in the outside world for the making of famous yaupon tea.

In this early village there lived a family of four: an ugly and evil-tempered matron, her two equally unattractive and evil daughters, and her stepdaughter, who was named Veronica. Veronica's father had been a seaman who, upon the death of his beautiful wife, had married this widowed matron in the hope of finding a peaceful home for himself and his young daughter.

Such peace was not to be.

When he could stand the constant nagging and vituperation of his second wife no longer, he gave her all the money he had and went to sea to try to build a fortune for his daughter's future. Contrary to what he had hoped, his plan turned out to be the worst thing possible for his daughter.

As the two ugly daughters grew older, they became more and more like their mother and assumed her unpleasant and scheming ways. Veronica, however, grew more graceful and lovely as she matured and was a very model of truth and beauty in contrast to her stepsisters.

This was a great cross for the stepmother to bear, and she responded in typically evil fashion. To Veronica she gave all the unpleasant, hard, and dirty tasks and the cast-off clothing of her own two daughters. In contrast, she pampered her own children by buying them clothes and jewelry with her husband's money and allowing them to perform the easy and pleasurable tasks around the house. But in spite of this treatment, Veronica continued to grow and blossom like a lovely flower, while the other two teenagers became more squint-eyed and mean of visage and disposition.

In desperation the stepmother decided to do away with Veronica. She did not, of course, want to do anything obvious that her husband could discover, so she consulted an apprentice witch who lived just outside Portsmouth Village for help in accomplishing her plans.

The fledgling witch was unable to arrange such a thing herself, but in exchange for several gold coins, she went into a trance and came up with a plan that seemed ideally suited to the evil purpose in mind.

On the southern end of Portsmouth Island, in a dense forest never visited by the townspeople or the sailors, there was said to live a mighty witch known only as the Sea Hag. She was supposed to be hundreds of years old. It was said that she had been driven out of Finland many generations ago by a brave priest and had fled to the new world to practice her profession.

And what a profession it was! Instead of riding a broom, she rode the long steering oar of a whaling vessel that she had caused to sink with all hands on board. The blade of the oar served as a sort of rudder in her airborne excursions. Now, this oar had no magical powers of its own. Like the brooms of many European witches, it drew its locomotive prowess from a salve which its owner concocted and rubbed into its surface from time to time to keep it charged and ready to go. The Sea Hag's salve was believed to be compounded of a mixture of deadly nightshade, monksbane, and hemlock, with a dash of poison ivy and cowitch vine, truly a witch's brew. This she was said to stir into a container of liquid fat rendered from some frogs and scorpions, which she kept for that purpose.

The Sea Hag was known to be always ravenously hungry. It was said she would eat children as well as the luckless seamen she was able to lure to their doom. If such a diet was not available, she was rumored to eat almost anything that came from the sea: porpoises, fish, crabs, stingrays, and sharks. This was the awful creature who was to be the instrument of vengeance in the freshman witch's plan.

Memorizing that plan to the letter along with a secret little spell that the apprentice taught her, the step-mother returned to her house and that very night put the plan into action.

Summoning the three girls, she bade them to card and spin and weave some wool into a fine woolen cloth for the approaching winter season. For this task she allowed them only one candle. Just as the girls were getting into their tasks, the candle by which they were working and every other candle in the house went out!

As her mother had instructed her to do, the older of the two ugly sisters upbraided Veronica and blamed her for the failure of the light. "Now we shall always have darkness," she said, "and we shall freeze in the coming winter." Taking her cue, the younger stepsister chimed in: "Now you must undo what you have done. You must go to the Sea Hag at her home in the dark south woods and beg her for light so that we may not all perish from your fault."

Veronica was terrified. She had heard tales of the Sea

Hag, and she knew that no one who had gone in search of her had ever returned. Her father was gone to sea, and she had no one to turn to in that bitter hour. She knew she must do what the stepsisters had ordered.

Now, the one thing that Veronica's father had given her before he left was a tiny doll. He had told her to keep the little doll with her always because it was a magic doll and had wonderful powers given to it by a good witch many, many years ago. The little girl had kept the doll as her father had directed, and it was through the help of this magical thing that she had been able to accomplish all the heavy tasks her stepmother had imposed.

Sobbing, the beautiful young girl felt her way in the darkness to her cold attic room and told the doll what had happened. "Do not fear," whispered the doll in its tiny, musical voice. "Keep me in your pocket and do as you have been told and no harm will come to you. I will help." So, tucking the little thing in her pocket, Veronica went down the stairs, out into the night, and into the dark and forbidding forest to search for the gift of light from the powerful Sea Hag.

On and on she stumbled through the underbrush. Often she stood stock still, chilled into motionlessness by the scream of some wild forest creature. When the dawn came, she went out on the beach and continued her journey until the blazing sun and her fierce thirst drove her again to the forest and the terror of the unfamiliar noises of the woods.

When darkness fell again, Veronica lay down on a soft bed of moss and slept fitfully until shortly before daybreak. Rising then from her forest bed, she drank from the dew accumulated in the leaves of a giant live oak and bravely continued her journey.

It was in that deepest darkness just before dawn that she struggled through an exceptionally dense thicket and came out into a little clearing in the woods.

There it was! There was the fabled home of the Sea Hag, more horrible than anything she could have imagined. The house itself was a small schooner that the witch had dragged into the forest after luring it ashore in a storm, but it had an after-castle in the manner of some ancient craft, which provided ample (even luxurious) living space. She could not see the inside of the cabin because it was surrounded with a fence. And what a fence! The walls of the enclosure were made of the bones of drowned sailors and fishermen, fused together by lightning into a solid wall of gray. At regular intervals along the fence there were taller posts made of the same material, and each pole was topped with a grinning human skull. The eye sockets of these skulls glowed with an eerie, orange light, which illuminated the clearing around the fence. As daylight broke across the forest, the light in those sockets faded gradually away and finally glimmered out entirely.

Just as the last spark disappeared, there was a great whistling noise like a strong wind, and in swooped the Sea Hag, riding her steering oar and singing in a high, cracked voice a sea ditty she had learned long before. Perched just behind the witch and seemingly enjoying the ride was an enormous black cat, bigger than any cat had a right to be. It was more the size of a wildcat, and its name was, in fact, Wile Catt. There was not a white hair on him, and his eyes glowed red like a live coal. The Sea Hag did not own him. He was his own cat, although he frequently went along with the witch on especially difficult expeditions to render aid and assistance when she needed it. Whether working singly or together, they always operated at night. A more fearsome pair you could not imagine.

In the pale light of dawn these two swooped down to a perfect landing inside the grisly fence. No sooner had they landed than Wile Catt's eyes blazed, his back humped up, and the hairs on his tail all stood up on end. Leaping from the oar, his eyes darting back and forth, the cat growled something in cat language into the ear of the Sea Hag.

"Oh ho," she cackled. "Mr. Catt smells the blood of a human. Come out, come out, wherever you are, or I'll call down the lightning your bones to char!"

Trembling like a leaf, our young traveller crept out of the woods and into the clearing, expecting at any moment to be eaten alive. "Come in, child, come in," snarled the witch. "Open the gate and come in." The hag pointed all the while at what appeared to be the main gate to the enclosure. Veronica had not noticed before, but now she saw that the latch to the gate was made of the gaping jaws of a man-eating mako shark. It was quite dead, but its razor-sharp teeth, which encircled the bone doorknob, looked as though they would snap shut at any second and sever the hand of anyone foolish enough to try to enter.

"Come in, child, or I'll give you to Wile," whined the old woman as she picked her teeth with the sting from the tail of a stingray.

Not knowing what else to do, the girl thrust her hand into the shark's jaws, turned the handle to open the bone gate, and walked into the witch's dooryard. Sobbing and wringing her hands, the young one told the hag the purpose of her quest, how all the lights in her stepmother's house had gone out and could not be relighted, and how she had been sent for the flame that would relight them.

"I don't know, human," droned the witch. "I've had a wonderful stingray stew or I'd eat you right now. I'm going to bed now, but when I awake at dusk I'll be hungry again before I start my night's work. You will find food in my house. Sweep and clean my house until it shines like the moon, and prepare me a meal before I awake, and maybe I won't eat you. In addition, out on the beach there are over a hundred trout that Wile and I scared ashore. Gather up those fish and clean them and scale them and have them ready for me to pickle. Do all this and I may let you live another day." So saying, the witch turned and disappeared into the rear of her little house.

Veronica tried to run away, but she found that she could not open the gate and the fence was too tall for her to climb. Defeated, she went fearfully into the witch's house. As the Sea Hag had said, there was plenty of food. The girl found some whole hams, a barrel of flour, several kinds of fish and shellfish, witch's cabbage, and many other things.

Sinking down upon the floor in despair of ever accomplishing even a part of what the witch demanded, she began to cry again and her nose began to run. She reached into her pocket to see if she could find a handkerchief, and her fingers came into contact with her magic doll. In all the stress of her journey and the terror of the encounter with the Sea Hag, she had quite forgotten that her little doll was there. Now she poured out her despair over her predicament to the doll. "Never fear," chimed the little doll as her tiny eyes sparkled with a kindly, reassuring light. "Lie down over there on that bunk and get a day's rest. I'll attend to the witch's demands."

The exhausted girl was only too glad to comply with her doll's suggestion and in no time at all was deep in slumber. She slept the day through, and when she awoke about dusk she found that her little companion had done every one of the things commanded by the Sea Hag. The house-ship was shining and as clean as a pin, and on the table was a gargantuan meal of selections from all the food in the place. Two hundred sea trout had been gathered up from the beach and cleaned and scaled and stacked in neat piles beside the brinetubs, ready for salting.

Just as Veronica was slipping the little doll back into her pocket, the door to the witch's bedroom flew open and the old crone emerged. "Is everything done, child?" quavered the hag in her high-pitched, cracked voice. Then she saw the table piled high with food and her eyes brightened with anticipation. Before she ate she made a detailed examination of her house. Not a speck of dirt or dust could she find. It was, indeed, shining like the moon.

"Well, I won't eat you just yet," she mumbled. "I've got a night's work to do, and if you want to stay alive another day, you must do some more things for me.

Cook me another meal even bigger and better than the one on the table and have it ready to eat when I return in the morning. In the backyard you will find fifty barrels of corn. Grind it all with the hand grinder and have the meal piled in a neat pile. Do this and maybe I will delay using your bones to repair my fence."

After eating every crumb of the huge meal, the Sea Hag climbed aboard her oar, and with a bone-chilling laugh, she zoomed out over the ocean just as dusk faded into darkness. Around the fence the eyes in the skulls gradually flamed brighter and brighter until they again lit up the scene. Wile Catt did not accompany the old woman on this trip. He was off attending to some personal cat business of his own.

Once again, the little doll performed all the tasks. Once again, as the dawn was breaking and the baleful, flaming eyes in the skulls were beginning to fade, the Sea Hag returned. Before she went to bed the old witch ate another tremendous meal.

Upon arising that evening, the hag again commanded the girl to do some impossible tasks. "Out on the beach," she snarled, "there are two hundred yards of my fish nets hung out to dry. Some naughty sharks got into them and tore great holes, and many of the floats and sinkers are missing so that they are of almost no use at all. Mend all the holes and repair the other damage, and cook me another snack like the others, and once again I may spare your life."

Upon her return, the Sea Hag found everything as she had ordered. After she had feasted again, she called Veronica to her.

"Girl," she said, "you make me nervous. I have given

you tasks that no human could perform, and yet you have done them all. Your magic is greater than mine, and I don't want to be around you any more. It can't be that witch-punk in Portsmouth. She's not even good enough (or bad enough) to change the direction of the wind or cause a ship to sink, much less do the things you have done. You say your evil stepmother and your ugly stepsisters want light from me? All right, I will give them light!"

So saying, she went out into her yard and chose a large, white skull from a pile there. Impaling the skull on a sharp yaupon stick, she handed it to Veronica and ordered her to begone and never to come back if she valued her life. Now, the fire in the eyes of this particular skull did not fade away with the increasing light of day but continued to burn steadily with a bright orange glow.

Grasping the stick tightly, the mystified girl carried her grisly burden to the gate, which opened wide for her, and she ran into the forest. When she had gone a short distance into the woods she stopped and looked for a suitable place to bury the thing. Suddenly a deep bass voice came from the skull. "Little girl, little girl," it said, "do not bury me. I am Lars Larsen, a Finnish sea captain the Sea Hag caused to drown many years ago. I may not rest until I have done her bidding."

Too scared now to do anything about discarding the skull-stick, Veronica continued to push through the thick forest. It seemed to her the underbrush was even more dense and harder to push aside, and the night noises even more terrifying, but she pushed ahead. Just as daylight was fading into night, she came at last to her stepmother's house. The entire house was dark. There was no light anywhere. As she opened the door and walked into the house, she was surprised to be greeted by the three ugly women with cordial smiles and greetings. The stepmother had gotten more than she bargained for from the apprentice witch. Ever since that first night no candle or lamp would stay lit in the house. Even lighted candles borrowed from the neighbors would gutter out as soon as they were brought into the dwelling, and no fire would burn in the stove.

As soon as Veronica told them that she had brought light from the Sea Hag as they had commanded, they began to laugh and clap their hands in joy. "Give me the light, give me the light this instant," begged the stepmother, grabbing for the stick topped by the skull with the glowing eyes.

Just as her hand closed on the stick, the light in the eye sockets blazed forth with an intense flare right at the stepmother. With a cry of pain, she jumped aside, but the skull turned on its stick until its eyes were again aimed at the old woman, and this time she burst into flame. She was entirely consumed by the fire, and all that was left was a little pile of ashes on the floor. Turning its head toward the two stepsisters, the skull completely burned them both until all that remained were two smaller piles of ashes. Then the light in the skull went out, but every candle in the house lighted up and filled the house with a warm, cheery glow.

Thus Veronica was rid of her tormentors, and the Sea Hag proved conclusively that she was far more powerful than the Portsmouth witch, who disappeared from the vicinity shortly thereafter. Some people say that the

Sea Hag got rid of her in order to cut down on any possible competition.

Veronica buried the skull on a stretch of deserted ocean beach, where Captain Larsen could hear his beloved sea breaking on the shore. She found a good home with a childless Portsmouth couple and more than earned her keep by helping with the housework and the chores. In time she married a fine young man who was a commercial fisherman, and they had a happy life together.

Some people said that the marvelous catches of fish they made were the work of the little magic doll her father had left her, but this was never proved. At any rate, Veronica kept the little doll safe and secure all her life and would let nothing happen to it. The belief is that the tiny magic doll is still in one of the abandoned houses in what is left of the town of Portsmouth, and that it is responsible for many of the wonderful things that happen from time to time on that secluded portion of North Carolina's Outer Banks.

THE DEVIL'S
CHRISTMAS TREE

*A*BOUT FORTY MILES almost due west from Roanoke Island as the seagull flies is the mysterious and beautiful body of water known as Lake Phelps. It is situated just off U.S. Highway No. 64, near the lovely little town of Creswell, and is the site of many colonial as well as ancient Indian legends.

In the 1830s an American patriot by the name of Josiah Collins II built a beautiful Southern plantation house on the shores of Lake Phelps as the manor house for his extensive land holding there. The state of North Carolina has had the excellent judgment to have the beautiful structure restored and refurbished just as it was in those days, with a marvelous view of the lake and long, tree-lined carriage roads. All of this accurate and detailed restoration is adjacent to Pettigrew State Park, and the stories and folklore about the estate, known through the centuries as Somerset Place, are legion.

One of those stories antedates Somerset Place by many years and takes place during the time when the very first English explorers and woodsmen began to penetrate this part of our country.

Very near where the plantation house now stands there was once an isolated trading post run and inhabited by an Indian trader known as Colonel Thomas Harvey. It was located near where the trading trails of the Iroquoian and Algonquian tribes crossed and was accessible to the small Siouan settlement located in what is now part of Pitt and Greene counties. Swapping trade goods for animal pelts and Indian artifacts, Colonel Harvey was able to show a very good profit when he made his periodic trips up to the settlements in coastal Virginia.

One of the colonel's occasional visitors was a hermit named Hercules Mann, an unusual fellow who lived quite alone in a hut on the extreme eastern shore of the lake in what is now Tyrrell County. Hercules lived entirely by hunting, fishing, and trapping interspersed with infrequent boat trips to the colonel's to trade for gunpowder, coffee, and rum, as well as other things he could not catch, kill, or fashion for himself. He was well known to the Indians of the region, who left him strictly alone as one "touched by the Great Spirit," or not really himself. Mann's boat was a typical Indian dugout canoe, which he had made by burning and chipping out the inside of a large juniper log and shaping the bow and stern until he had fashioned a very serviceable craft. He propelled the boat with a rather long paddle, which had a flattened blade at one end and a blunted point at the other. When he traversed the shallow waters near the shore, he would pole the boat with one end of his paddle, and when he was in deeper water he would use the flattened or paddle end to drive the craft forward.

His only companion was his dog, a canine of uncertain ancestry that he had trained from puppyhood as a deerhound. The dog was an excellent trail dog and more than earned his keep in helping with the hunt and in protecting his master from the bears and various other wild animals that showed an interest in Hercules' dwelling and in the venison, the sun-dried fish, and the Indian corn, squash, and beans he kept for sustenance.

One bitterly cold Christmas Eve, Hercules decided that he would like to have a nice Christmas dinner of fresh venison to go with his Indian vegetables, so he called his faithful dog into his dugout canoe, took his rifle and hunting knife, and set out across Lake Phelps toward the western shore more than five miles away. As he paddled, the wind increased out of the northwest and a considerable chop began to build on the lake, making it more and more difficult to drive the little canoe along. With the wind chill factor added, the man and his dog grew even colder, and they were frequently splashed with spray from the building waves.

By the time they reached the far shore, it was quite late in the afternoon and had begun to snow, first with small flakes and then larger and larger, as an ominous-looking cloud bank to the west loomed closer. The snow did not particularly bother Mann, though, since he was used to the hardships of severe weather in his lonely life as a hermit and he especially wanted a nice buck for his Christmas celebration.

Securing his little boat against the freshening off-shore wind, Hercules called his dog and they set off into the woods in search of their quarry. In a comparatively short time the hunter heard the familiar sounds of his dog "giving tongue" in a high-pitched, almost hysterical voice as he gave chase to some animal. Then came the welcome noises of a deer crashing through the undergrowth and heading almost directly toward the hermit. With every muscle tense, Hercules went into a

126

half crouch and raised his rifle to his shoulder, pointing in the direction of the approaching noise.

With a tremendous leap, a huge buck deer sprang into the clearing and stood stock still just a few feet from the hunter, its nostrils flaring as it confronted the man with the gun. The huge animal was snow white from the point of its nose to the tip of its tail, and its antlers spread to an incredible breadth. It seemed not at all afraid of the human before it.

Aiming carefully at the vital spot just behind the deer's shoulder blade, Hercules pulled the trigger and fired. He took half a step forward, expecting his quarry to fall dead at his feet. The hunted took two steps toward the hunter and fixed him with a threatening glare, then turned and walked majestically off into the forest, his antlered head held high, his white tail flickering in the fading light.

Just as the deer disappeared, Mann's faithful dog came panting up and looked all around as though completely bewildered at the absence of his prey. The hermit was shaken. How was it possible for him to have missed at so close a range? What worldly deer would have moved menacingly toward him after the rifle blast? He sat down, trembling, in the snow and tried to figure it out. Not a hair on that deer had moved. Not a muscle in the animal had flinched. And yet it had been at point blank range and he was a skilled marksman. Shaking his head in disbelief, he turned to comfort his disappointed dog and found him begging in his canine way for another hunt—another chance at a deer.

Knowing it was getting later, and acting against his

better judgment, Mann gave in to the pleading dog and set him off on another hunt. Once again the familiar music of his dog's trailing voice gladdened his ears, and once again he heard the crashing in the undergrowth. This time a small red deer came bounding out of the woods. With one clean shot at the fast-moving target, Mann killed his deer.

It was too late now to dress the deer out on the spot. The light was fading fast and the snowfall was increasing by the minute. Dragging the still-warm carcass into the boat, the hermit called his dog aboard and set out with the wind at his back for the long return trip to his hut on the opposite shore.

Once again the spray from the wind-driven waves splashed into the boat. But now it was freezing as it fell, and the carcass of the deer became icy and stiff. Huddled against his dog for warmth, the hunter drove his small and heavily laden boat toward home as fast as his strength would permit, pausing every now and then to bail out his boat before the water from the spray could freeze solid beneath his feet.

When he was about halfway across the lake and as he stopped once again to bail, he was astounded to hear a loud crack of thunder in the midst of the heavy snowfall. Immediately thereafter a large blue light appeared in the sky, lighting up the surface of the water all around with an eerie glow. The brilliant light appeared to descend slowly toward the water and to grow brighter as it neared.

Now, Hercules Mann had heard about St. Elmo's Fire, which had frightened sailors for generations by playing along the upper rigging of their ships and giving the appearance of flames along the sails, and he earnestly hoped that this was what he was seeing. Frightened out of his wits by all these strange occurrences on Christmas Eve, he redoubled his efforts and soon reached the little wharf in front of his hut.

Beaching his boat, he dragged the stiff carcass of his deer up to the front door of his hut and called his dog to stand guard over the prize while he went inside to build up his fire and prepare to dress out the deer on the rack nearby. He paused only briefly to warm his hands over the rekindled fire before carefully laying out his dressing knives on the table. He then went out the door to string up the deer on the dressing rack.

His deer was gone!

His faithful dog was nowhere in sight.

Mann knew that the dog would have sounded the alarm if anyone or anything had come up while he was in the hut and would have put up a whale of a noisy fight if any animal had tried to steal the deer, but there had not been a sound. He had been in the hut only a very few minutes. The hermit called and called his dog, but there was no answering bark. The forest was completely silent, and the large snowflakes continued to drift slowly to the ground.

Suddenly the eerie blue light flared again, lighting up the hut and the surrounding opening with the brilliance of a full moon. Hercules Mann looked around him in a sort of daze. There were no footprints of any kind and no sign that the carcass had been dragged away. The surface of the snow-covered ground was without sign or mark, except for a few drops of what appeared to be blood leading into the dense woods to the north. Following this scant trail of blood illuminated by the mysterious light from above his head, the hermit pushed his way through the underbrush until he was several hundred yards from his home.

As he cleared an especially dense thicket, there was another clap of thunder and the blue light grew brighter. There before Mann's startled eyes was a large cypress tree, and about it danced a horde of swamp spirits, moaning and shouting, "He shot the white deer, he shot the white deer, the devil will claim him for aye and a year." As they danced and flew around the large tree, he could see that they were decorating it like a huge Christmas tree. As they went from limb to limb they hung long icicles on each branch, and the frozen decorations immediately lit up with all the colors of the rainbow, and they glowed with a strange fire of their own. Then, just as the cypress seemed to be completely covered with the lights, there came a burst of crimson light from the very top of the tree. There, hanging from the highest branch, suddenly appeared not a star, not a cross, not the figure of an angel, but the ugly face of Satan himself, an evil grin creasing his sinister face.

Mann fell to his knees, his body shaking uncontrollably, staring in shock and disbelief at the apparition.

At that precise instant, the scream of a Carolina cougar split the winter air. Every light vanished and once again complete silence reigned in the forest. With a groan, Mann struggled to his feet and ran clumsily back in what he thought was the direction of his home. He stumbled into the lake and fell flat on his face but managed to rise again and finally followed the shoreline to his hut.

Terrified, with his clothes freezing on his body, he ran to his boat and frantically began to pole the craft up the shoreline in the direction of Colonel Harvey's trading post. It seemed an eternity before the lights of the shack came into view and he was able to slam his boat into the wharf and stumble through the door, falling on his face just inside.

Colonel Harvey gave him immediate treatment. He stripped the frozen clothing from the shivering, babbling man and wrapped him in a bearskin rug. Building up a roaring fire in the fireplace, he massaged the hands and feet of his guest and gave him several large shots of rum to drink.

As soon as he had stopped trembling from cold and fear, the hermit told the colonel of his experiences. Gulping down hot soup and boiled venison the trader pressed on him, he began to talk more and more slowly, until at last he dropped off into a deep sleep before the fire.

Christmas morning dawned bright and clear, and Mann was anxious to be off for his hut again to look for his dog and to see if he could find any explanation for the happenings of the previous evening. Despite the protests of the trader, who told him that he was not well and should not overtax his strength, Hercules insisted on leaving. Thanking the colonel again and again for his kindness and with a good, hot breakfast in his stomach, the hermit pushed off in his dugout and headed for home, promising to return and bring the colonel any clarification of what he had seen and done.

The trader promised to wait Christmas dinner for him and watched him until he was out of sight from the wharf, poling his little boat briskly down the lake.

Morning turned into midday, and midday faded into afternoon, and still the hermit had not returned. Giving up on his guest, Colonel Harvey ate a hurried and belated Christmas dinner alone and then started out in his own canoe in search of the man. It was almost dark again before the colonel reached Mann's dwelling and found there not a sign of the hermit.

Inside the hut everything was in order. The fire had long since gone out, but the dressing knives were there, lined up on the table just as they had been left. There was no sign of any violence or any struggle.

Lighting his hunter's lantern, the trader looked about outside the hut and there picked up the footprints of his friend in the snow. There was only one set of prints, and they led off into the forest in a northerly direction. There was no sound except the crunching of Harvey's boots into the snow as he followed the trail by the light of his lantern and of a full moon above.

Several hundred yards away from the cabin the trader found his friend, kneeling in the snow in front of a large cypress, his eyes open and staring in death as though he had died gazing in disbelief at that tree. There was not a mark on his body with the exception of the figure "666" burned into his forehead as though with a red-hot branding iron.

"My God," whispered the trader. "The mark of the beast—the devil's own."

Somehow Colonel Harvey was able to drag the body back to the hermit's hut and place it in his boat, with which he was able to transport it back to the trading post.

With the help of some Indian friends, he gave the hermit a Christian burial the next day and placed a wooden cross at the head of the grave. All during the preparation of the body for burial the Indians continued to point at the figure burned into the pitiful forehead and to ask, "Who did? Who did? What mean?" Colonel Harvey gave them no answer. He only shook his head sadly and went about his task of directing the burial.

So ends the story, as far as we know, of Hercules Mann.

If you have opportunity to visit the restored Somerset Place, it would be well worth your time to do so. You will feel that you are stepping back in time to the days of long ago, and the past will suddenly become more real to you.

Do not look for the trader's station, however, nor for Mann's hut. They have long ago gone the way of all buildings that are uncared for. If you are lucky, you may find one of the older residents of the area who will tell you that the huts may be gone, but the devil's Christmas tree appears every Christmas Eve night, and if you listen, you can clearly hear the hermit and his dog in pursuit of a deer. If your eyesight is good and your heart is in tune, you can also see the rainbow-colored lights of the tree glimmering and reflected in the calm waters of Lake Phelps. Never, never, never try to approach it. You don't want to wind up, like the hermit, with your forehead branded with the devil's sign.